HEART OF THE SERPENT

Born in North Middlesex Hospital on 25 September 1961, Thomas Bloor has lived for most of his life in various parts of the London Borough of Waltham Forest. He took a degree in Fine Art at North-East London Polytechnic and has worked as a school librarian, an art technician, a classroom assistant and an artificial flower maker. He now does some part-time teaching and editorial work but devotes most of his time to writing. He currently lives in Walthamstow with his wife, two daughters and two cats.

Heart of the Serpent completes the trilogy that started with *Worm in the Blood* and continued with *Beast Beneath the Skin*. *Worm in the Blood* won the Calderdale Children's Book Award 2006 and was shortlisted for the Highland Children's Book of the Year Award and the Bolton Children's Book Award.

www.thomasbloor.co.uk

Also by **Thomas Bloor**:

WORM IN THE BLOOD
BEAST BENEATH THE SKIN

'Utterly gripping . . . Stirring, original stuff.'
Independent

'A great idea, beautifully set up and explained.'
Herald

'Bloor has woven myth, fantasy and harsh reality into
this riveting story.' *Carousel*

'An edgy but hugely gripping cross-over children's
book.' *One Life Magazine*

HEART
OF THE
SERPENT

Novel and illustrations by
Thomas Bloor

ff

faber and faber

First published in 2007
by Faber and Faber Limited
3 Queen Square London WC1N 3AU

Typeset by Faber and Faber Limited
Printed in England by Mackays of Chatham plc, Chatham, Kent

The right of Thomas Bloor
to be identified as author of this work has been
asserted in accordance with Section 77 of the Copyright,
Designs and Patents Act 1988

A CIP record for this book
is available from the British Library

ISBN 978–0–571–23495–0
ISBN 0–571–23495–X

2 4 6 8 10 9 7 5 3 1

Thanks to James, the originator of the Cheese Bean Special, for his horticultural advice. Thanks also to Elaine and Kathryn, and to Julia Wells for her work in editing this book and its two predecessors.

In memory of my father
David Clifford Ernest Bloor
(1924–2006)

I

Voice of the Rain

RESTING PLACE

The corpse lies deep and undisturbed. All life has long since departed. Marsh grass waves solemnly over the boy's last resting-place. A keen wind bends the rushes. Rain lashes the pools of murky water that surround his grave. Nothing can touch him now.

The boy's remains bear the evidence of several wounds, for his end was not a peaceful one. But when the body fell into the waters of the marsh, it sank too deep and too quick for raven, rat or blowfly to make their mark. So what was once, a great many years ago, the living body of a fifteen-year-old boy, now lies still and silent beneath the preserving soil.

The wet earth packed close around his lifeless flesh has seeped into every pore, inhabited every cell. The natural chemicals in the liquid mud have kept the body intact. It hasn't decayed. There has been no return to dust or dirt. Instead, the earth has protected this particular human frame. The marsh has some other purpose in mind for the long-dead boy. Soon, this body will see the light of the sun once more.

SOMETHING LOOKED

The girl put one foot on the garden path. The straggly grass shivered, the dead rosebush trembled in the chill wind. Old crisp bags and burger wrappers shifted uneasily on the overgrown lawn.

'Go on!' She heard the jeering voices of the other two, her friends waiting at a safe distance, back behind the burnt-out car on Sew Road. 'Look in through the window. Do it!'

The front door was facing her. Scuffed and stained and covered in graffiti, but an ordinary door nonetheless. The only odd thing was the pile of broken stones and concrete that had been heaped against it. Someone didn't want that door to open.

'Go on! Look inside!' All she had to do was walk up the path, lean across the rubble and look through the narrow, grime-covered window next to the front door. She took another step. Then another.

The wind blew, bringing with it a hint of rain. A loose section of guttering grated against the brickwork with a sound like fingernails on a blackboard. The girl swallowed. She was going to do it. Then they'd have to give her all their sweets for a week. That was the deal. She'd show them. She hated her friends. Pressing her face against the filthy windowpane, the girl looked into the house.

In the gloom, something moved. Something looked back.

The girl's screams echoed around Sew Road. The sound of her trainers clattering along the path and away down the road, with her friends close on her heels.

A magpie perched on the roof of the derelict house, amidst the loose and broken tiles, and uttered the harsh series of clicks that it passed off as song. But the thing inside the house remained quiet and still. It closed its eyes and tried to forget.

ALONE AND IN DARKNESS

Sam watched her drown. Adda-Leigh, suffocating, choking, dying in front of his eyes, and there was nothing he could do to prevent it.

She was under the water. Her mouth was open, her lungs flooding. Her limbs flailed, but her movements were sluggish and slowing by the second.

Sam kicked furiously, thrashed his limbs and twisted his body, he even beat his wings against the unyielding depths. He had to get to her, had to save her. But the water held him back. Water, that had been his salvation, the element in which he felt most at home, now turned against him. No matter how he tried, he couldn't move.

And while he struggled, Adda-Leigh drowned. Her head tipped back and her eyes opened. She gazed sightless at the surface of the water far above. A shudder convulsed her body. Her braided hair floated about her head. Her arms spread, she drifted, gently floating. Beams of light pierced the gloom of the water and lit the sea in glowing shafts all around her. And she hung there, suspended. And she was an angel. And she was nothing. And she was dead.

Sam howled. His anguished yell boiled and bubbled, stifled in the dark and salty water. The shout woke him at last. His whimpering, nightmare-wracked voice broke through the thin wall that divided sleep from waking. He opened his eyes and groaned. He was alone, lying stretched out on a reeking, mildewed carpet inside a derelict house. Alone and in darkness.

He swallowed, and the foul taste of burnt bile caught in his throat. Adda-Leigh wasn't dead. She hadn't drowned. That was no dream of the past. None of it had happened. But his relief was only temporary. The nightmare was recurring. He'd had it before, night after night. And Sam was afraid it was a dream that told of things to come.

ON THE INSIDE

'Sam?'

There was a long pause. The phone line crackled and buzzed with static. There was a sound like sand being poured into a bucket. Then a voice spoke, faintly, as if heard from far away.

'Georgette . . . Have you . . . spoken to her?'

There was no need to ask who the voice was talking about. This was Sam.

It was remarkable that she could hear him. Georgette doubted he could even speak at all now. The voice she heard on the telephone was the voice Sam had spoken with a year ago, back before the changes. Back when he was still human. What Georgette was hearing was Sam's thoughts. He was able to send words formed in his mind via mobile phone masts and satellites and landlines. And these thoughts were delivered through the voice of a teenage boy. A boy who no longer existed.

So he must still be human on the inside. Georgette shivered. Sam was trapped. Trapped inside the body of a monster. It was a terrible thought.

'*Have you spoken to Adda-Leigh?*' There was a catch in Sam's voice as he uttered the name, as if it caused him turmoil just to allow those syllables to form in his mind.

'Yes. On the phone. I'll be seeing her soon, when I go down to London.'

'*When?*'

'Half-term.'

'*What?*'

'Next week.'

Half-term didn't mean much to Sam any more. He may still have been a boy inside, but he was a boy who hadn't been to school for a year, who'd been living alone for half that time, who'd seen and done terrible and wonderful and impossible things. As she listened to the static shift and swirl on the line, Georgette wondered how much of the old Sam was really left.

'*Is she . . . ? How is . . . ? Is everything . . . ? Did she . . . ?*'

Georgette couldn't help but smile. Sam may have changed but the way he felt about Adda-Leigh was as painfully obvious as it ever was.

'I don't know why you don't just talk to her your-self. She wants to hear from you!'

'I just . . . I don't . . . I can't . . .'

'All right, Sam. Stop now. Be quiet, please. Adda-Leigh's fine.' Georgette sighed then went on. 'Listen to me. I'm changing the subject. I have to talk to you. About the Order. I'm worried about them coming back, coming after us again.' She paused for a moment and swallowed. 'I've seen one of them.'

The Order of the Knights of the Pursuing Flame were a secretive organisation, not easily spied on. They had already existed undetected for hundreds of years, waging a war of extermination against the dragon-folk of Luhngdou, an isolated island in the South China Sea. Sam was believed to be the last living soul of Luh-ngdonese descent, the last to carry the dragon-folk gene, and the last to undergo the transformation from human to dragon. The Order had killed all the others. They were very good at killing and they were very good at keeping out of sight. And yet Georgette had seen one of them.

'I won't let them sneak up on us again, Sam! I won't!' She gripped the receiver hard as she spoke, first remembering how Adda-Leigh had gone missing for weeks, and then thinking of a night six months before. The night they got her back. A night of fire.

It was the smell of burning that had stayed with her.

The sight of the church in flames, glowing red against the dark sky, the sound of the tower collapsing and the clamour of the falling bells, these memories she was able to block out. The smell of burning was harder to shift. She couldn't forget the fact that Master Richard and Ishmael had both died inside the blazing church.

She had no reason to mourn their deaths. It was the thought of breathing in smoke containing particles of their charred remains that upset her. Master Richard and Ishmael had been at the heart of the Order, as its leader and its most potent warrior. They'd kidnapped Adda-Leigh, Georgette's best friend, and held her captive for weeks. They'd wanted Sam to fight and die at their bidding and had come close to making this happen. Georgette had little doubt they would have killed her too had the fight gone their way.

But it hadn't. Georgette had found Adda-Leigh and together they'd watched while a winged, fire-breathing creature that had once been Sam fought with the sword-wielding Ishmael. Ishmael and Sam had been the same age. Fourteen years old. They shared some of the same D.N.A. They'd fought each other to a standstill nonetheless. Georgette would never really be able to forget the scorched air, the flicker of the flames, the blood-spattered gravel outside the church, or Ishmael's fire-blackened sword, thrust point-first into the ground.

Others had witnessed the battle. Selected members of the Order. Georgette remembered the clipped, military tones of one man, though she hadn't seen his face. Another witness she knew already. Crisp, a racist and a killer, a man she'd seen shoot down an old woman in cold blood. That night he lay broken and grovelling in the dust. All at the sight of Sam, wings spread, hovering in the air, plumes of fire darting from his jaws.

What had happened to these other witnesses, to the surviving Knights of the Order? They'd all fled into the night. All except Ishmael and his master. Their deaths would have been a terrible blow to the Order, but would it have been a fatal blow?

The question might not even have occurred to Georgette if she hadn't seen the man.

Two weeks ago Georgette had been in London on a flying visit to see her father. While he was driving her to the station for her journey back to York she'd seen, or thought she'd seen, a man she recognised. He was huddled in filthy blankets, peering out of a shelter made from wooden pallets and damp cardboard, pitched underneath a concrete footbridge. Despite being in the passenger seat of her father's car, passing the bridge at speed, she'd still recognised him from that single glimpse. It had been Crisp.

'It was him. I'd swear to it. Up near King's Cross.

That's not far from Marshside. Not far from Adda-Leigh's house.'

'He's been trailing me for weeks.'

Georgette paused, taken aback.

'And you've waited until now to let us know? So why is he in Marshside? You're in Wales, aren't you?'

There was an awkward silence.

'It's my fault. I'm back in London.'

'And what does he want?' Georgette's voice was cold. She was angry.

There was another pause.

'He wants to kill me.' Sam said. Then his voice was swallowed by a surge of static and the dragon logo on the phone display panel flickered out.

DYING WORMS

The earthworm writhed on the walkway, drowning in a few millimetres of chill rainwater.

There was little enough earth on the Coldferry housing estate for worms to live in. Just the gritty soil in the bottom of a few concrete planters. The planters were home to some dying gorse, and plenty of old drinks cans and discarded plastic bags. So the worm wasn't local. It had fallen from the sky, dropped from the beak of a careless blackbird as it passed over the estate from the leafy gardens of the nearby terraced streets. Only two beings knew anything of this slow, watery death. One was the worm itself, and the other was the creature that had once been Sam Lim-Evans. Nothing passed Sam by. Even the death of a worm reverberated through his consciousness like the tolling of a tiny bell, sharp and cold and insistent.

The dragon-boy had stayed away from London as long as he could. And he knew he shouldn't have come back. He ought to keep away from everyone he knew. But he was so alone he could hardly bear it. Even though he didn't dare meet up with Adda-Leigh, at least here he was close to her, under the same grey sky, breathing the same London air.

Sam lay in a dank and unlit passageway, behind the barricaded door of the derelict house on Sew Road. This was the border of Coldferry, a bleak no-man's-land between the newly built council flats and the older, well-to-do drives and avenues not five minutes' walk away.

Ruptured water pipes had flooded the ground floor, and overflowing drains had spilled their contents into the empty home. The water had been cut off, eventually. Nobody lived there. Just Sam.

Outside, a pest-control worker sat in his van talking to his head office on a mobile phone. Sam's hearing was so sensitive he could hear the man quite clearly.

'No. I can't get inside. Someone's dumped a load of rubble in front of the door. Must be fly-tippers.'

Sam knew that a man across the street had called in the pest-control firm. He'd caught a glimpse of Sam, slipping over the garden fence. And the man couldn't believe what he'd seen. He told himself it was a fox. A very big fox. He'd called pest control. As for the pile of rubble, that wasn't fly-tippers. The old lady next door had got her son to heap the doorway with gravel and broken bricks.

'I just know there's something nasty in there,' Sam had heard her say. 'I don't want it getting out.'

The pest-control man was afraid. Sam could hear it in his voice.

'To be honest boss, this place creeps me out. I keep getting the feeling something's watching me.'

Sam closed his eyes as the van pulled away. His mind, however, was open to all that went on around him. Telepathic visions constantly flickered across his consciousness. And it was the bad things that stood out in sharp focus. Anything from frightened pest con- trollers and teenagers brandishing kitchen knives, try- ing to slice each other up in the echoing stairwells of the low-rise flats, to a humble earthworm, dragged into the air and then dropped on the ground to die in a puddle of icy rain.

And still it was better to let these endless testaments to the negative side of life run through his mind than to allow himself to brood. He had been an ordinary fourteen-year-old boy. Now, just a year later, he had lost everything.

His father was in Wales. They hadn't spoken since

the changes. The only person who had really understood what he was going through, a priest named Father
David, was dead. He had no home, no possessions. He
had nothing.

All vestiges of human physique were gone. He
couldn't stand upright any more. He slithered on his
belly. A pair of powerful, leathery wings were folded
against his back, all skin and sinew. His body was puckered with scales, its surface so rough that a piece of
cloth drawn repeatedly across his back would be
snagged and torn to threads within a few minutes.

His face, once human, with just a touch of something pleasingly unusual inherited from his half-Welsh,
half-Oriental parentage, was now distorted beyond all
recognition. His jawbones were stretched and elongated into the muzzle of a beast. Needle-sharp teeth
crowded his gums in snaggling rows. Recognisable
human speech was impossible. Guttural sighs and low
moans were the best he could manage. Through days
and nights of agonising mutation, his heavily muscled
torso had become longer and leaner. His limbs now
seemed short in proportion to his body. Worst of all, a
sinuous serpent's tail had developed. It was now several
metres long, emphatically inhuman, a final, terrible
indignity.

He was a monster, a reptilian thing. A serpent. A
creature, through and through. He was something

slimy and grotesque, hiding under a rock. How could he ever see Adda-Leigh again, now he had degenerated so far? He couldn't even bear to talk to her on the phone. And yet, if he allowed the telepathic visions of knife fights and dying worms to falter for an instant, he found he could think of nothing but her.

Was Adda-Leigh in danger again, because of him? Crisp was quite mad, Sam was sure of that. But the man had never been more than a foot soldier of the Order. So was Crisp alone, his quest to track down Sam no more than the final twitching of the corpse of the Order? Or was he still part of something larger?

Sam knew he couldn't stay cooped up in a derelict house for ever. He had to find out what was left of the Order and what, if anything, it was planning. He had to find Crisp. He was Sam's only lead. But, as he breathed in the damp air of the derelict house, Sam wondered if it would be Crisp who found him first.

BACK

Adda-Leigh looked at the sky. The boundless space. The infinite void. Whether lit by the sun, the moon, the reflected lights of the city at night, or, as now, covered in a layer of low grey cloud, she loved it. Adda-Leigh loved the sky.

Every time she left the house her expression would lighten. It was just so good to get out, to walk in the fresh air, be it cloudy and grey or clear and blue. Staying indoors was never easy for her these days, and small confined spaces were intolerable. Recent experiences had left her with a bad case of claustrophobia. Just thinking about using the Underground brought her out in a sweat.

Underground. That's where they'd held her prisoner. Master Richard, who had ordered her capture. Ishmael, who had been her jailer. And all to act as bait. It was Sam they'd wanted. The Master had been determined that Sam should die. And Ishmael had been willing to do anything Master Richard told him. Adda-Leigh knew that in a way the strange and damaged youth had meant her no harm. But what would he have done if Master Richard had ordered her to be killed?

Adda-Leigh shivered at the thought and thanked her stars she was no longer trapped and powerless, imprisoned underground. She had the cold air of a chilly February morning to blow the memories away.

The rain had stopped, for a while at least. She set off, out through the gate and down along the road, her braided hair swinging about her shoulders. The heels of her pointy-toed boots tapped out a rhythm on the pavement as she walked. With an iPod earphone in her right ear and a silver earring dancing from the lobe of her left, she strode along, her step keeping time to the music she was listening to.

She pulled an apple from the pocket of her coat and crunched into it as she walked. She smiled. There was a sadness in her eyes but the look didn't linger too long.

A crowd of secondary-school children in grey uniforms were hanging around the bus stop on Iron Ferry Road. Marshside kids. Dressed all in blue, Adda-Leigh click-clacked past them. She'd switched schools in the autumn and had further to go to get to St Michael's. Her parents had wanted her to make a fresh start. The kidnapping had been traumatic for everyone concerned. For Adda-Leigh, her family, her friends, even her school. It was time to put it all behind her, if she could.

Some days were better than others. Today felt like a good day. It was the Friday before half-term. Georgette would be here by the time she got back from school, down from Yorkshire to visit. Adda-Leigh took one last bite of her apple then, without a glance, threw the core into the large round street bin next to the bus stop. The core sailed straight in without touching the sides.

STICKS AND STONES

The man was grey with grime. His face was all bone and tight-stretched skin. His cracked lips were drawn back over his few remaining teeth. His yellow tongue darted from side to side, like a snake tasting the air. He held out a dirt-blackened coin in the palm of one emaciated hand.

'A pound!' His voice was as rough as his appearance. 'A pound to anyone who'll tell me who lives in that house!'

In the gloom of the derelict property, Sam's eyes snapped open. He'd been sleeping, lost in a nightmare of the past. His anxious dreams had blotted out the sixth sense that had been warning him of his enemy's approach. But now he could detect the presence of the man outside. And he was close. Sam could hear him now, through the walls of the house, talking to a crowd of kids who'd been playing in the road. There was no mistaking his cracked tones. Crisp had tracked him down once again.

'So who piled them bricks and stuff in front of the door?' The man's eyes were wild, bloodshot, glittering with violence and fear. 'There's something strange in that house, isn't there? Tell me!'

The children looked at each other. They were tough street kids, but the old house made them uneasy, and this ragged lunatic was scaring them too.

'Two pound!' he said, pulling a second coin from his ripped pocket. He stretched out his hands, palms open, beseeching.

The first stick came sailing over the children's heads, from somewhere at the back of the little crowd. The man was hit on the head. He flinched and bared his teeth, drawing back. The coins dropped from his hand.

More sticks were thrown. And stones, swiftly gathered from the pavement.

The man turned and ran, stumbling, his arms held up to protect his face. The children followed slowly, at a distance, waving sticks and throwing dirt and grit. They stopped when they saw where he was heading and watched as he disappeared around the back of the derelict house.

Inside, Sam saw that Crisp was heading straight for him. He'd listened to the violent clamour outside and now he was gripped by nervous indecision. Adrenalin boiled through his blood. He felt fire building in the back of his throat and he drew his clawed hands across the floor. He was ready. Fight or flight. But which should he choose? If he left it too late the decision would be out of his hands. Even now, he could sense Crisp, standing at the back of the house, looking for a way to break in.

Crisp was a killer. Crisp was a madman. Crisp's mind burned with an intense hatred for Sam. The man's life had spun out of control since he'd first stumbled upon the secret war between the Order and the dragon-folk and their allies. Now he was lost, a broken, homeless obsessive, doomed to wander the streets of London searching for monsters. And here it seemed he'd tracked the dragon to its lair.

Sam could read these thoughts as they spun through Crisp's confused mind. The dragon-boy gave a snort that left a plume of yellow smoke twisting in the dank air. Then he lunged forward across the rotted floorboards.

A HOMECOMING

The train pulled into King's Cross Station and Georgette turned away from the rain-streaked carriage window. She'd spent the journey down from York watching the fields and farmsteads give way at last to the dark and crowded streets of London. Although she didn't live here any more it still felt like coming home.

The bus ride from the station to Marshside was quicker than she remembered it, with the driver making the most of the lull in traffic just before the school run began. Georgette decided to meet Adda-Leigh at the gates of St Michael's School. She took the short cut past the estate. As she passed the junction with Sew Road she saw some kind of incident was in progress.

Two police cars, their lights flashing, were parked in

the road by a burnt-out car. A crowd of kids were watching. A few adults too, arms folded, staring. An officer was looking up at a derelict house.

Georgette couldn't help but glance over. Someone had piled a heap of rubble by the front door. There were shouts, a scuffle. Two policemen emerged from the side of the building holding on to a man, who struggled and yelled.

'It's inside! Let me go! It's inside! Don't you under-stand? I have to kill it!'

Georgette stopped. She stared. Crisp. Again.

He was in a terrible state. Filthy, emaciated, raving. But there was no doubt. It was him.

And now he'd seen her, too. He lifted his head as the police dragged him to their waiting patrol car. His struggles intensified.

'There! There's one of its friends! Her! That girl there! She's an enemy of all of us humans! Arrest her, not me!'

The crowd turned and stared at Georgette.

'Don't listen to him, love,' one of the policemen called out to her. 'He's not well.' Then he turned to the crowd at large. 'Move on now, please. There's nothing to see here.'

Still shouting, Crisp was steered into the back of the police car, a constable's firm hand pressing the top of his head.

Georgette turned and hurried away but Crisp's hoarse shouts rang out behind her.

'Monsters! Reptiles! Dragons! I'll kill you! I'll kill you all!'

SEWER BOY

Sam might have known he'd be found. He'd been careless. Neighbours had seen things they couldn't explain. A dark shape slithering through the rubbish-strewn garden. Something large. With wings. Something no sane person could believe in. They'd dealt with it in their various ways. There'd been talk. Even so, it seemed extraordinary that Crisp had found him. He was never far behind. Crisp was a man obsessed.

He'd first tracked Sam down in the forest that lay beyond the suburbs bordering Marshside. Sam had been lying low, deep within the woods. But Crisp had found him there. And Sam had fled.

In some ways, he was running from himself. Sam knew what he himself was capable of and it terrified him. Crisp was a constant reminder of that fact. He'd been there at the fight at the church. He'd seen Sam defeat his enemies, seen how close he'd come to tearing their throats out. And like his memories, Crisp wouldn't leave Sam alone.

A wild kicking at the back door. The splintering of rotten wood as the frame gave way. The stumbling footsteps. Crisp's bellowed shout, 'Beast! Demon! Alien! Show yourself!' His voice was twisted and choked by the madness that had him entirely in its grip. Sam had heard it all. But he was no longer there.

Several days before, he had taken the precaution of tearing out a section of flooring and digging his way into the main sewer that ran beneath the house. So when Crisp kicked his way in, Sam was already submerged in effluent, moving slowly away through the filth and darkness of the tunnel. He had no need of air to breathe or light to see. By the time the police were bundling Crisp into the back of the patrol car Sam was several streets away.

And yet he was still not too far away to hear what was happening, nor for his sixth sense to register a familiar presence in the vicinity. Georgette.

He moved on in the fetid darkness of the sewer. Panic-stricken rats swam from him. For a brief moment the terrified rodent shoal formed an involuntary honour guard. Then, with a flick of his tail, Sam swept on past them all.

Uneasy thoughts spun round his head. If Crisp had been acting alone, then his arrest would be an end to Sam's troubles. But if the Order were involved then not only Sam but his friends too could be in danger.

Would there never be an end to it? For a year now, Sam had been tracked by friend and foe alike, pursued from the marshes of north-east London to the forests of southern Ireland. And there had been casualties.

Crawling through the filthy sewer, Sam felt a familiar dull ache in the pit of his stomach. Misery. At least Crisp had a purpose, to hunt Sam down. At least the Order had an aim, to rid the world of Sam's kind. But what of Sam himself? What was the point of him? He moved on through the stench and the darkness. But no answer came to him.

The North-East London Gazette

MARSH BODY PREHISTORIC SAY EXPERTS

The sensational find of a body buried in local marshland, at first thought to be the victim of a recent gangland killing, is now believed to be a far older case of murder most foul. Police were called in when workmen carrying out repairs on the Marshside reservoirs discovered the body of a young man buried deep in the mud. But after examination by a pathologist the police contacted the Museum of London. A spokesman from the museum confirmed their involvement. 'This is an exciting discovery, the first of its kind in the London area. The body is in a remarkable state of preservation, due to the chemicals in the marsh mud. It could be thousands of years old.'

A team from North-East London University, including some of the country's leading experts on human archaeology, is on its way to examine the find. A police spokesman commented that, given this victim's estimated time of death, they were unlikely to be making any arrests in relation to the case.

GUARDIAN ANGEL

Georgette looked at the gates of St Michael's School. Old. Wrought iron. A crest, cast in relief and picked out in glossy colours, was fixed below the pointed tops of the railings. An armoured knight with angel's wings, trampling a writhing dragon beneath his heels.

'Don't blame me for the school badge.' Adda-Leigh jerked her thumb at the gates. 'I could have screamed when I saw it. It's not just Saint George who killed a dragon, you know. Plenty of other saints got in on the act too. Including Michael. But I won't wear a school jumper with that badge on it. I don't care if they do keep sending me home for being out of uniform. That badge is not for me.' Adda-Leigh threw her arm around her friend's neck. 'It's good to see you, girl!'

Georgette patted Adda-Leigh on the shoulder

awkwardly and ducked under her arm. She wasn't one for hugs, even from her closest friend.

Smiling and shaking her head, Adda-Leigh set off along the pavement and Georgette fell in beside her.

'Sorry,' she said. 'It's good to see you too. Seeing Crisp again like that, it gave me a fright, that's all. The police were dragging him out of some derelict house.'

'He's been arrested?'

'I suppose . . .'

'So that's that. He's out of the way. I almost feel sorry for him. The man's not right in the head.'

'I wouldn't waste any pity on him. He's a racist and a murderer and he tried to kill you! I'm sure no one would blame us for hating him, even if he is a bit touched!'

Adda-Leigh stopped walking and looked Georgette in the eye.

'I still get nightmares. But they're not as bad as they were. For the first time in months I'm feeling better. I'm not going to let Crisp get to me. He's just a sad old nutcase.'

Georgette coughed. 'The thing is, Addy, what if Crisp isn't the only one still out there?'

'Georgette. Nothing's happened. We're all fine. Okay you've seen Crisp a couple of times but now he's been arrested so –'

'But what if the Order still exists?'

'Can't you forget about that for a while?'

'I can't help it.' Georgette looked at the pavement. 'I know it was awful for you, getting kidnapped and everything, but it wasn't exactly all fun and currant cake for me either. It's not so easy to just forget everything that happened. Maybe I'm paranoid, but I can't help thinking it might happen again. And if there is something creeping up behind me I'd rather know what's coming.'

'Not sure I would. I'm more a hide-beneath-the-bedclothes sort of girl myself.' Adda-Leigh turned away and started walking, but her expression suddenly brightened. 'We've got Sam though, haven't we? I know I haven't seen him for a while but he's always been there for us in the past. I think he knows when we're in danger. Sort of senses it, or something. He's like our very own guardian angel.' She giggled. 'He's even got the wings!'

Georgette had to force a smile. Adda-Leigh certainly knew how to put on a brave face.

She thought of the image on her friend's school badge. St Michael, crushing the dragon beneath his heel, his face a mask, devoid of any emotion, his eyes cold. She couldn't help wondering if there were more survivors of the Order out there, still obsessively pursuing the last of the dragon-folk and all his associates. And, if that proved to be so, whether the protection Sam could offer would always be enough.

NIGHT ON THE MARSH

Sam left the shadow of the railway embankment and headed out across the marsh. He always came back to the marsh.

Clouds hid the moon and rain was falling steadily. Lights glimmered, up on the flyover. The grumble and hiss of passing traffic was a constant background accompaniment to the sounds of the marsh. The place was alive with wildlife. Sam listened. He felt cold and alone.

Coiled beneath the dense and twiggy branches of a sprawling hawthorn, he struggled to calm his thoughts. He was restless and his recurring nightmare made him wary of sleep.

He looked through the mesh of twigs, out towards the winking street lights beyond the canal, over in the direction of Adda-Leigh's house. She was there, at home, doing ordinary things. Eating dinner, chatting to her mum, listening to music, reading a magazine.

It was a calming thought. Sam's breathing slowed. If he was calm he could will himself into total stillness. And then he was able to become almost completely invisible. No danger of being seen, of hearing people scream in terror at the very sight of him. No one but an expert steeped in the lore of Sam's ancestors, the Luhngdonese, could see around this screen of invisibility. Father David had been one. A good man, a guide and mentor, he'd tried to help Sam cope with the terrors of the transformation. But he was gone now. Dead. Killed by the Order.

Sam was still. Immobile. He wasn't breathing. Not the faintest shiver or twitch. That, together with something else, something intangible powered by an unconscious sensor at the back of his mind, a signal he sent out to baffle any potential onlookers, made him virtually impossible to see.

Through his deathly stillness, Sam's mind continued to function. He would send a voice message to Georgette's mobile. Someone should know what he was planning to do. He couldn't face contacting Adda-Leigh or Aaron, his old schoolfriend. At least with Georgette they'd never really been close. Somehow that made it easier to cope with talking to her.

But there were times when any human contact would just serve to remind Sam of how lonely he was. He decided to delay tapping into the frequency until he could be sure Georgette's phone was engaged or switched off. He prepared his message in advance.

The police will have taken Crisp back to where he escaped from. It's a place called Stoneberry.

There'd been flashes of Stoneberry in the wild fragments and images Sam's extra-sense had picked up when Crisp had got close to him. An institution. A secure unit. Stoneberry.

I'm going to have to go there, Georgette. I don't know what's going on with Crisp. I hope there's no more to it than there seems. He's totally lost it. He believes he has to kill me. To rid the world of monsters, or whatever his messed-up mind is telling him. He's sick and twisted, but I don't want to hurt him. He doesn't even have to know I'm there. If I can just get close enough, and give myself the time to properly read his thoughts and his memories, I'll be able to tell for sure if he's still a part of the Order. If he's not, it could mean they don't exist any more. Or it could just mean Crisp has broken away from them. It won't tell us much, but it'll be a start at least. I have to do something. I'm afraid something might happen. To Adda-Leigh. Something bad. So I'm going to Stoneberry. I might have to stay there a while.

Stoneberry. A cold name, but with a twisted sweetness to it. Old-fashioned. Respectable. Pleasant sounding. But Sam had the feeling there would be nothing pleasant about Stoneberry Mental Hospital.

THE FRAGMENT

Glamwych Reservoir – North Wales

The wind rippled the surface of the water. Sister Ironspeare stood before the hidden door. It was concealed in the undergrowth and perfectly camouflaged, invisible to the casual observer. But Sister Ironspeare knew it was there.

Through the doorway a long flight of steps led down to a small, damp room. Condensation dripped from the ceiling. Banks of computer screens flickered and hummed. It wasn't a pleasant place to work, and yet she'd spent many, many hours there.

It had all been worthwhile. The fragment had yielded up its secrets at last. The words had been the easy part. Medieval French was one of the many dead languages

Sister Ironspeare was fluent in. So she had known from the day she found it, on a library shelf in the derelict wing of a crumbling château, that the fragment referred to her. It spoke to her by name. It promised to tell her what her future held. The others, fellow members of the Order of the Knights of the Pursuing Flame, had believed the fragment too. They had fallen in behind her. She was their leader now. The fragment had made that happen.

But what did it mean? And where was the rest of it? Those questions she had answered at last, after days and days of tireless research. The fragment was part of a secret book. The Book of the Last. This book contained the final prophecies. The Masters of the Order had declared the book heretical. They had denied its very existence. And yet she, Sister Ironspeare, would find it, and it would tell her what she had always believed. She was born to greatness.

But there was more. The fragment spoke of how the book would reveal the final destiny of the Order itself. It would speak of the glorious day their mission to rid the earth of the dragon-folk would at last be complete. All the other texts the Order held sacred had promised them great power when their mission was over. The Book of the Last, it seemed, told them exactly how and when it would happen.

Sister Ironspeare was convinced that soon she

would know the location of the Book of the Last. With her followers at her side she would seize the book and the final glory would be theirs.

Standing at the water's edge, she turned her face into the chill of the wind and allowed herself the barest flicker of a smile. It was a smile not of pleasure, not of happiness. It was a smile of triumph.

TEA OR COFFEE

The windows of the cafe were streaming with condensation. Outside, it had started raining again. The two girls were the only customers.

Georgette coughed. 'I'll be seeing my dad tonight. He's taking me out to eat somewhere. But he'll drop me back at yours later.'

Adda-Leigh said nothing. She picked up her cappuccino then put it down without taking a sip.

'Georgette. Do you know where Sam is?' She kept her eyes on her coffee cup as she spoke. 'He's been in touch, hasn't he?'

'I was going to tell you.' Georgette tapped at the rim of her steaming teacup. 'You know the reason he won't talk to you, don't you? He likes you too much.'

Adda-Leigh sighed. 'That boy is such an idiot some-times! So where is he?'

Georgette was silent.

'What? What is it?'

'He's gone to find Crisp. He wants to know what's going on. He thinks there's some kind of danger.'

'What danger? Who's in danger?'

'He wasn't sure. He said . . . He thinks it's you.'

Adda-Leigh rolled her eyes. 'I'm in danger. Again. Fine.' She twisted her cup around on its saucer. 'Maybe he just wants an excuse to rescue me. That's the only time he can bring himself to actually see me!'

A silence fell between them. At the counter, the coffee machine gasped and wheezed. A radio played, the sound low and crackly.

'That's what happened to the phone messages he left me,' Georgette said, nodding her head towards the counter. 'They start out fairly clear, but you can't save them. They just fade away until you can't hear anything but radio hiss.'

Adda-Leigh darted Georgette a look. 'Do you think he'll ever . . . you know . . . turn back?'

Georgette didn't say anything. After a while she shrugged her bony shoulders. She took a sip of her lemon tea and grimaced. 'Too hot!' She blew into her cup.

'You don't, do you?' Adda-Leigh said. She sighed.

'I'm sorry.' Georgette shook her head. 'How do I know what to think? A year ago the whole transformation thing would have sounded impossible. In fact, it still does! It's impossible, but it's real. We've seen him change. But the changes only seem to go one way.'

Georgette fell silent and looked down at her tea. Adda-Leigh lifted her coffee cup to her lips. In the background the radio played a corny ballad of lost love. But the tune and the lyrics were indecipherable, drowned out beneath a wash of static.

CLOUD SKIMMER

Sam skimmed the vaporous cloud tops. Wings outstretched, he glided through the thin air. Ice formed on his scaled skin, and yet he felt no cold. His mind whirred and his body was forgotten.

Down through the cloud his destination waited. On a wooded hillside in a dull suburb north of Marshside stood a sprawl of brick buildings and crumbling prefabs surrounded by a high wall. Stoneberry Mental Hospital. Most of the old Victorian wards were empty now. The inmates had been moved to other smaller, more up-to-date units, or released into community care. The empty corridors awaited the final closure of the hospital and the arrival of the bulldozers. But one corner of the old site was still in use. The Stoneberry Secure Unit. It was from here that Crisp had escaped, once before. And it was where he had been returned. Sam could sense the man's presence, even from so far above. His stomach heaved. Crisp made him feel sick.

Folding back his wings, Sam dived, spiralling out of the night sky. As he swept downwards he closed his eyes and let his mind reach out, in through the walls of the secure unit, searching out the thoughts and memories of those inside. If he could isolate Crisp's mind, and tap in to it to find out all he needed to know, then his stay at Stoneberry might only be a short one.

Sam was relatively new to mind reading. Over the past six months, his extra-sensory powers had continued to develop, as had his physical prowess. But his psychic abilities were much harder to control. There was little consistency to what he could and could not do. And without Father David to guide him, Sam could only improvise and hope for the best.

He realised that he'd made a mistake almost immediately, but by then it was too late. There were very few inmates left in Stoneberry Hospital. Those that remained, however, were the most dangerous and unstable of patients. Their dreams and memories twisted in the air of the unit like a great and terrible swarm. As he hurtled towards the ground, Sam was confronted by a clamour of images that burst into his mind from all sides. Screams, dreadful whispers and unearthly cries rang in his ears. He saw flashes of things he would never have wished to see. Twisted agony and fury, desolation, despair and a boundless desire to inflict pain boiled through his mind in a scalding wave. Overcome by horror, Sam slipped into unconsciousness. Out of control, spinning in a wild tangle of limbs and wings, he continued to fall.

CALLING HER GEORGE

'Did you get my text?' Georgette was talking to Aaron on the phone. She paced up and down the pavement outside the curry house, her mobile pressed to her ear. A few metres away her father waited by the restaurant door. He stood stamping his feet against the cold, his large frame silhouetted against the illuminated menu displayed in the window behind him.

'You need to know what's going on. You have to watch out. I've seen Crisp. Twice. He was hanging around near Adda-Leigh's school. Sam thinks something's going on.' She lowered her voice. 'With the Order.'

'Steady on, George. Calm down.' Aaron sounded unconcerned.

'Don't tell me to calm down!'

'So Sam's back, is he? And he's back to normal, yeah?'

'Aaron! You saw him yourself! You saw what had happened to him!' Georgette lowered her voice. 'You saw what he'd become. Of course he's not back to normal!'

'I saw — I don't really know what I saw. To be honest, George, I sometimes wonder if I dreamed the whole thing!'

Georgette lowered her mobile phone. She held the handset at arm's length and glared at it furiously. Aaron was an idiot! She'd forgotten how angry he made her. She put the phone to her mouth again and spoke, with a forced calm.

'Well, don't say I didn't warn you. And, Aaron, please do not call me George!'

She stabbed the end-call button so hard she bent her fingernail back.

Behind her, her father gave a cough. 'Finished, love? Boy trouble, is it?'

'Don't. You sound like Mum.'

'Sorry.' He looked down and shuffled his feet. 'Look. I can't pretend to know about your life. But whatever you've got going on, you know I'm always around. If you need any help. If you get into any kind of lumber. I'm your dad, after all.'

Georgette looked at her father. She didn't want him

involved. The thought of him tangling with a madman like Crisp and being fished out of the canal with a bullet through the head filled her with a sick horror.

'Don't worry about it, Dad,' she said. 'I'll be fine.'

'Good. Now, are we going to eat, or what?' His voice was tired. Somehow he looked a lot older than the last time she'd seen him, only a few months ago. 'When you were on the phone, you'd forgotten I was still here, hadn't you?' There was wry amusement in his voice, but his eyes were sad.

'No. Of course not.' Georgette hurried over to him and slipped her hand into the crook of his elbow.

In the curry house, while her father ate lamb vindaloo and drank Cobra beer and waved his fork around as he talked about his plans for opening his own bar and restaurant in South London, Georgette sat toying with her naan bread. He'd got the evening off work to take her out to dinner while she was staying with Adda-Leigh. They'd got the bus on Gunpowder Row, he was paying for dinner and later he would take her back to Adda-Leigh's house before heading for his own place, a couple of cold and uncomfortable hours away by bus and tube. Was it true, what he'd said to her outside? He was her father, and she didn't see him often. But still, when she'd been thinking about Crisp and Sam and the Order, she really had forgotten he was there. The realisation made her feel sick. Would she ever be able to put the past behind her? She laid down her half-eaten naan bread and pushed her plate away.

WORLD TURNED UPSIDE DOWN

Sam opened his eyes. Twisted twigs and branches hung above a dark and cloudy void. There was a ceiling, hung with lush grass. It was above his head, where the sky should have been. The world had turned upside down.

It was a moment before he understood what had happened. He'd fallen into the branches of a tall tree in the grounds of Stoneberry Hospital. The tree had broken his fall. His torso was wedged into a crook in the branches, his tail twisted around the trunk. He was dangling, with the top of his head just above the ground.

Sam groaned and shifted, swinging backwards and forwards, dislodging himself, gingerly. His body ached all over. Uncoiling his tail from the tree trunk, he slithered to the ground, landing with a gasp and expelling a jet of grey smoke from both nostrils. Broken branches and snapped twigs lay scattered in the long grass. His descent had clearly not been a gentle one, but at least he seemed to have come out of things rather better than the tree had.

Sam shook his muzzle from side to side to try to clear the buzzing from his ears. He had survived a fall that would have killed him outright, back before the changes took hold of him. Even as recently as six months ago he might have been much more seriously hurt, although his recovery would have been swift. Now, he had a bruise or two and he felt a little groggy, but otherwise he'd escaped unscathed.

Physically, it seemed he was becoming almost indestructible. His mental well-being, however, was another matter. He remembered the wave of psychic anguish that had caused him to pass out, and he shuddered. He would have to use all his strength to block out the thoughts of the inmates here at Stoneberry. And he would have to get close enough to Crisp to be able to select which part of his mind he was going to read. And the only way to do that would be to get inside the building.

THE WATCHER AT THE WINDOW

Adda-Leigh was sitting in her room, gazing out through the windowpane into the darkness of the night. She heard Georgette come in but she didn't move.

'You okay, Addy?'

Adda-Leigh didn't reply at once. 'The marsh is out there. That's where Sam went when he first started to change.' She shivered. 'I tried to get our history teacher to take us down there on a class outing. But he wouldn't, the boring old fart. They found some dead caveman down there, apparently.'

'It made the national newspapers. He was from the Iron Age. The son of a chieftain, they reckon. Killed as a sacrifice, or something. And he wasn't a man, he was a boy. Well, a teenager, in fact.'

'Like us.'

'Yeah. Like us.'

'I just want to see him. That's all.'

'Well, I hear he's going to be put on display in the Museum of London sometime.'

'Not the dead caveman, silly, I mean Sam. I want to see Sam.'

Georgette was silent for a moment. 'Don't you remember what he looks like these days?' she said, quietly.

'Don't, Georgette. I don't care what he looks like. I miss him. I can't help it. And I know it's stupid. I hardly knew him when he was . . . you know . . .'

'Human?'

'Whatever. But now, with the things we've been through, everything that's happened this past year, I don't see how I can go back to normal life again. How can I ever like an ordinary boy after all this? It's Sam or no one. And what if something happens to him? He shouldn't have to stay wherever he is, all on his own.'

'He's a giant reptile with supernatural powers, Addy. If anyone can survive out there it's Sam.'

Adda-Leigh was silent for a while. 'But no one should have to be alone,' she said at last.

INSIDE STONEBERRY

The lawn in the hospital grounds hadn't been mown in a long time. Tall grass lay in straggled clumps, soaked by the rain. Sam was pressed flat against the ground, still, silent and invisible. Ahead of him was the compound of the secure unit. Harsh spotlights blazed down on the walls, bleaching them a hard, bone white.

He'd been in the grounds of Stoneberry Hospital for two days and two nights, watching, biding his time, getting to know the routine. This evening, he'd decided, he was going inside.

He'd contemplated simply storming the building. He was certainly strong enough to break down the walls and force his way into Crisp's presence. But how much damage would he inflict if he did that? There could well be physical injuries, even the deaths of innocent people, not to mention the psychological damage it would inflict on the already vulnerable individuals here at Stoneberry. No. Sam knew he had to enter and leave by stealth.

He heard the van approach along the roadway that ran from the main gate to the entrance to the secure unit. The sprawling branches of the overgrown shrubs squealed against the sides of the van as it drove past.

Sam rose up, kicking at the ground. His wings beat once, twice. He glided over the long grass in the darkness, silent as a hunting owl.

There had been kitchens at Stoneberry, but they'd been closed down. It wasn't seen as cost-effective to cook meals on site for the small number of inmates that still remained. Instead, food was brought in from the nearest general hospital, stored in a heated meal cart. A catering assistant wheeled the food around the rooms of the ward, distributing meals. He didn't know it, but tonight Sam would be accompanying him on his rounds.

The catering assistant, who also drove the van, laboriously unloaded the meal cart and pushed it up a concrete ramp and into the unit. There were two sets of double doors. He left the first doors unlocked and pushed the meal cart up to the second door, by which time Sam was inside. Spreadeagled against the corridor walls, his heartbeat suspended, his great bulk was undetectable.

He listened to the man breathing as he worked, droning a tuneless melody through his nose, jangling the keys that swung from a fob on his belt. Sam listened, but he made sure he wasn't in touch with the man's thoughts. He'd been practising keeping at bay even the slightest of mental disturbances from the mind of another. He knew that once he got inside the secure unit, one slip-up could be disastrous.

It wasn't difficult to gain entry. By alternating swift, silent movements with periods of stillness and invisibility, Sam followed the catering assistant past the security guard, who sat nodding at his desk, and the male nurse, busily writing up some notes. No one was expected to try to break in to the secure unit. All the security systems were designed to keep the patients from getting out.

The ward consisted of a number of locked rooms and a central corridor. But in which of these rooms was Crisp to be found? A harsh strip light illuminated the corridor. Sam, pressed against the wall, felt horribly exposed, despite being sure he couldn't be seen. He realised he would have to use his mental powers to identify the right room.

Taking a deep breath, he opened his mind to the thoughts of the people in the building, and then, as quick as he could, he shut off his senses again. It was like a psychic blink. But it was enough. It was almost too much. He began to shake as the twisted power of that split second of combined mind-reading juddered through him. But now he knew where to find Crisp.

He waited until the care assistant was by the door of what Sam now knew to be Crisp's room. The man was struggling with the heavy meal cart, grunting with exertion as he tried to force the wheels to turn the way he needed them to. Behind his back, Sam was in plain view, convulsed with tremors, stretched out on the floor, desperately trying to recover his composure. The huge scaly creature with wings was utterly out of place in the sterile and brightly lit hospital. But the assistant didn't look back. He unlocked the door and, leaving the meal cart outside, he went in.

Sam dragged himself along the corridor and followed, slipping through the door before it swung to. He pressed himself against the wall, desperately shutting down his senses and forcing his laboured breathing back under control.

The care assistant turned back to the meal cart in the doorway. The patient lay in his hospital bed.

'Evening, Mr Crisp. How are we today?' A plate of food was put on a wheeled tray, and pushed into place over the bed. 'It's lamb cobbler tonight.'

Sam remained as still as stone. But he was struggling to stay in control. The strain of being in the hospital, so close to such troubled minds, was breaking down his defences. He felt a pulse twitch in his throat.

Crisp raised his head. His movements were slow. He blinked, as if trying to focus.

'I've gone and forgotten your fork, Mr Crisp. I shan't be a mo.'

The care assistant shuffled out into the corridor to where he'd left the meal cart. Moving slowly, Sam approached the bed. But it was no good. His concentration slipped. His mind was assailed by a terrible combination of wild emotions that seemed to emanate from the very bricks of the secure ward, as if years of mental distress had become stored up in the walls of the building. He gasped and retched, arched his stomach and was sick, vomiting hot embers on to the polished floor.

'Monster!' Crisp's cry was slurred. He struggled to sit up in bed. 'You've made a big mistake, coming here! Now I've got you, you alien!' He snatched up his spoon and flung it hard. It bounced off Sam's muzzle then clattered away into the corner of the room. Sam rolled on to his back and took a deep breath. The care assistant appeared in the doorway. Sam pressed himself back against the wall and remained stock still. He shut off his heartbeat.

'Oh dear, oh dear, oh deary me. What have we done here? Got a bit of a dicky tummy have we, Mr Crisp?'

Crisp was swinging his arms feebly. 'Show yourself, dragon!'

'I'll get a mop and a bucket. Looks like hospital food don't agree with you.'

Crisp glared at the care assistant then pointed a trembling finger at the pool of black and steaming vomit. 'That wasn't me. It was the dragon.'

'Course it was.' The care assistant turned and shuffled out of the room, locking it behind him. He returned moments later with a mop and bucket. Sam remained frozen in invisible stillness. Crisp continued to stare groggily around the room.

'There we are, Mr Crisp. All the nasty dragon sick's been cleared up now. You get a good night's sleep and I'll see you on me next shift.'

The catering assistant left the room a final time, and once again, he locked the door behind him.

'No one believes me.' Crisp's voice was soaked in bitterness and self-pity. 'But I've seen them. Dragons. Alien scum! They're here. We have to get rid of them!'

He slumped back on the bed, exhausted. The medication took hold of him. His eyes closed.

Sam approached the bed. He looked at Crisp. Small and emaciated, all the hatred had drained from his face. In deep unconsciousness, with his mind swept blank, Crisp looked almost childlike. Although his thoughts had shut down, his memories would be intact and Sam had to get to them.

He raised one clawed hand and flexed his long, large-jointed fingers. He laid his palm against Crisp's dry forehead and closed his eyes.

He pictured a small, almond-shaped area of the brain, the seat of memory. Sam had nothing but his instincts to tell him where to look and how to avoid all the lies, delusions and fantasies that lay entwined with the memories. But at last he found what he'd been looking for.

LONG LIVE SISTER IRONSPEARE

Crisp barely remembered the place or the time. It was somewhere he'd been taken to, not so very long ago. Sam, reading the memory, had only the vaguest impression of surroundings and no idea of a location. As for the company, most of the faces of the people in the room were no more than a watery blur. But Crisp remembered the woman.

Her name was Sister Ironspeare.

The room was full of blaring chatter. The sound was echoing in Crisp's head. His temples were pounding. The talk was of the Order, of the old Master, now dead. The tone was smug and foolish.

'Well, Master Richard always said that . . .'

'Master Richard,' an icy voice interrupted, cutting through the sudden silence in the room. 'Master

Richard was a fool. He came close to destroying the Order. Look how he left us, our resources drained, our agents scattered. And he allowed the last of the dragon-folk to escape. For that blasphemy he cannot be forgiven, even in death.'

The speaker was a woman. She was dressed in a grey habit, like a nun. Her hair was hidden beneath a tight wimple. Sister Ironspeare. Crisp knew her name, though no one had uttered it. The woman's face seemed ageless. Smooth-skinned, and yet not youthful. Taut and stretched, but with no sign of weakness.

'Since Master Richard's death we have had to regroup. Those of you here tonight have all answered the call. But there have been others who showed reluctance to continue the struggle, who asked for money, or a position of power, before they would carry on serving their Order. They have been dealt with. The major is a man of vast experience in such matters.'

A man in his fifties, sporting a neat moustache, his lean, tanned features criss-crossed with wrinkles, gave a long-toothed smile and bowed his head. This man Crisp also knew.

'The end result', the nun continued, 'is a leaner, fitter Order. Knights all, and all of us willing to fight for the power that shall one day be granted us. Look around you, my friends. We happy few, we are the Order! What finances remain, have been pooled. We know what we must do. We must take Streaming Point. We must find the Book of the Last.'

Sister Ironspeare held up a torn triangle of a stiff, yellowing, parchment-like material covered with an ornate hand-written script.

'This fragment is from the Book of the Last. It is all I have been able to obtain from this most secret of the Order's treasures and it took the deaths of many knights for me to come by it. These few lines prophesise my rise to the leadership. It was written over one thousand years ago, and yet I am named in it as "The Lady of the Iron Spear". The rest of the book will reveal our destiny. It will explain how we, the Order, can claim the power on earth that we have all come to expect. The Order has a future far beyond the extermination of the dragon-folk. When the last of that cursed race are dead, we shall take up our true position as rulers of the earth. And the Book of the Last shall reveal to us how that will be achieved. It will chart our future, and it will be glorious.

'For centuries now, the Masters of the Order have known of the existence of this book. And yet it has remained hidden, unread, a secret among secrets. They have been determined to keep the vital knowledge it contains to themselves. But that is not my way. The Order may be fewer now, but we are hungrier for power! Let us take the hidden hoard of Streaming

Point for ourselves, wrest the Book of the Last from the lifeless hands of the traitors who guard it, and discover the true path at last!'

The memory became hazy now. It was the first time Crisp had encountered the woman whom he saw as his leader. Master Richard was dead. Long live Sister Ironspeare.

But it wasn't the only time he'd met her. There was another memory. More recent. Again, the place was impossible to identify. Just a room. Windowless. Dimly lit. A sound of water, dripping. A stale smell to the air. But Crisp remembered the name of this place and to Sam it sounded familiar too. Glamwych. Where had he heard that before?

Crisp may not have remembered much about the room, but he remembered who was in it. Sister Ironspeare was there and she spoke to Crisp, her cold, watery eyes fixed on his.

'I'm giving you one last chance to show your loyalty to the Order. Find the monster,' she told him. 'Find it, and destroy it! I can help you locate him. But it must be your quest, your one purpose in life. You must hunt down the beast. You must slay the dragon and anyone who knows of his existence. His family. His friends. The world must be wiped clean. And if you fail, you will forfeit your life.'

BEAUTY SPOT

Sam shivered. It was past midnight. He'd been crouched there, looming over Crisp in his hospital bed, for hours now. He was exhausted, nauseous and gripped with anxiety. And he felt disgusted at what he'd done.

He'd broken into a mental hospital and rifled through the memory of one of the patients, a man who was lying drugged in bed, powerless to resist. The fact that the man was Crisp, a known killer who wanted him dead, didn't fully excuse him. Neither did the information he'd managed to extract, which he hoped would help him to protect himself and his friends. There was still something about breaking into another man's memories that made him feel like an interrogator, a torturer even. He felt wretched with guilt.

Silver moonlight streamed into the ward, casting a striped shadow across the floor from the barred window. He wondered if he could tear out the bars without raising the alarm. He hesitated. Sam wanted to get out as soon as possible, but he didn't really want Crisp to be able to escape too. It was clear now that Sister Ironspeare had encouraged Crisp's obsession, had ordered him to pursue his own demented agenda, his relentless hunt for Sam. If there'd ever been a chance for him to recover his sanity it had gone now. Crisp would pursue Sam to the ends of the earth. His life depended on it.

Sam turned his attention to the door. Using one slender claw as a tool he began to chip away at the wood. If he could cut out the lock he'd be able to slip out unseen. But the need for silence meant working very slowly. He couldn't think of any alternative, but still he wondered if he'd make it out of Crisp's room before the shift changed at six o'clock.

An hour had passed. There was a small pile of sawdust on the ground. Crisp was shifting restlessly in his bed as the effects of his medication began to wear off.

Sam stopped what he was doing. He had the feeling something was about to happen. A threat was approaching. All his senses tingled in anticipation. He leant his body against the door and peered out through the small window of reinforced glass. Forcing his pounding heart to slow Sam faded into invisibility. He watched the corridor.

After a while he heard some sounds he couldn't identify. A few soft thuds and muffled reports. Then, at last, something happened. An intruder appeared. He was dressed in black combat gear, and carried a handgun fitted with a silencer. He was bareheaded. Sam recognised him from Crisp's memories. This was the man Sister Ironspeare had referred to as being an expert in assassination.

The man in black made straight for Crisp's door. Sam retreated into a shadowy corner and froze once more just as the door burst off its hinges and the intruder entered the room. Crisp sat up, surprise and alarm on his gaunt features.

'Major?' he said, his voice a hoarse croak.

'Yes,' said the intruder in a clipped, military accent. 'It's the major. Get up.'

The major changed the ammunition clip in his gun while Crisp struggled out of bed.

'What are you doing?'

'Switching to live ammo. Don't need tranquillisers now.' The major smiled, the wrinkles spreading around his eyes, creasing his whole face. He seemed to be a man who enjoyed his work.

Sam watched as the major left the room, with Crisp stumbling along at his side. He slipped out after them, crawling along the corridor, his wings folded against his back, keeping as low as possible. The time for concealment was over. Something was very wrong at Stoneberry Secure Unit.

At the end of the corridor the staff of the night shift, two security guards and the male nurse, were slumped around the nurses' station. Sam's senses told him they weren't dead, just unconscious, shot with the major's tranquillisers.

Sam froze at the far end of the corridor and watched while the major opened his rucksack and pulled out three half-empty whisky bottles.

'Finishing touches,' the major said. 'Can't have suspicions raised. Must keep everything hush-hush.'

He tipped the contents of one bottle over the unconscious men. Then he reached back into his rucksack and pulled out a children's party hat. He looked at the nearest of the two guards. He snapped the elastic hatband under the man's chin. The tiny party hat was perched on the guard's lolling head.

'Time we were off.' The major seized Crisp by the arm and dragged him out through the double doors and down the concrete ramp. Sam followed as soon as he dared. If he could trail the major without being spotted then he might be led to the rest of the Order, perhaps to their new leader, Sister Ironspeare. If he knew where to find them he could monitor their movements, keep ahead of them at all times, and discover how to escape their attentions once and for all.

Having manhandled Crisp up and over the perimeter wall using a rope ladder and a small grappling iron, the major drove him away in a black jeep. Sam took to the air and followed, flying low at around a hundred metres, keeping below the heavy cloud so he could keep track of his quarry. It was the early hours of the morning and the jeep was one of the only vehicles on the road. Sam didn't lose sight of them until they disappeared into some thick woods on the northern edge of London.

He landed on a rubbish-strewn stretch of gravel at the side of an empty road. The major's jeep was nearby, parked beneath some spreading oak trees next to a man-made lake. Beyond the lake the woods stretched away into darkness. By day this was no doubt considered a local beauty spot. The sort of place parents took their children to feed the ducks. But in the dark hours before dawn it was desolate, with no houses nearby and no passing traffic.

Sam slipped through the trees, moving as silently as he could. Using his sense of smell, he tracked Crisp and the major through the dark of the forest.

He found them in a copse of beech trees beyond a small clearing on the far side of the lake. Crisp was on his knees. The major stood behind him, with the barrel of his gun pointing at Crisp's head.

'Sorry, old boy,' he said. 'Needs must and all that. Shouldn't have let the police pick you up. Shouldn't have blabbed to all the head-shrinkers about the Order.'

'But nobody believed me!'

'Not the point. Now pipe down, there's a good man. Time to meet your maker.'

'Wait! Please! Take me to Wales. Take me back to Glamwych. Let me see Sister Ironspeare.'

'I'm acting on her orders, old thing. She told me to make it look like you escaped and then topped yourself in the woods. Now, no more chit-chat. Cheerio.'

The major's finger tensed on the trigger. Sam, watching in horror, now began to move rapidly through the trees, beating his wings and clawing at the ground. He had no thought of what he was going to do. But he knew he couldn't stand by and watch a man get murdered. It was as if something deep inside him made him protect Crisp, almost against his will. This man had been tracking him for months, had been on a mission to kill him and all his family and friends, but still he couldn't leave him to die. He burst into the clearing and felt the flame rise in his throat.

'Who's there?' The major spun around and pointed his gun straight at Sam.

Sam opened his jaws wide and let the scream that had been building up inside him come bursting out. A sheet of flame spewed from between his lips, lighting up the beach trees with a sulphurous yellow glow as it blazed across the ground towards the major and Crisp.

NIGHT CALL

Georgette woke with a start. She glanced over at
Adda-Leigh, fast asleep in her bed on the other side of
the room, lying on her back with her mouth open and
looking a lot less glamorous than was usual. The room
was lit by a shaded lamp because Adda-Leigh couldn't
sleep in the dark.

Georgette stared up at the ceiling and wondered
why she'd woken at three in the morning.

Then her mobile rang.

She reached out and grabbed it off the bedside cup-
board, pressing the answer key and stifling the ring
tone before it woke anyone up. Georgette looked at
her phone. The dragon logo was flickering wildly on
the display.

'Sam?'

Through an even thicker blanket of static than usual, Georgette could just about make out Sam's faltering words.

'I . . . They . . . I saw . . . It was . . .'

'Sam! What's the matter?'

'Georgette . . .' Sam's voice was firmer now, but wracked with suppressed pain, as if he was forcing himself to concentrate. *'The Order. You were right. They haven't gone away.'*

'What happened, Sam? Tell me!'

'He escaped . . .'

'Who? Crisp?'

'Yes. And the other one. But I think I . . .'

'Other one? Slow down, Sam. Start at the beginning.'

'They talked about Glamwych. They've got some kind of HQ there, I think. And there's a place called Streaming Point that they're interested in. They're planning something, though I don't know what. But that's not all. They still want us dead, Georgette. You, me, Adda-Leigh, Aaron. My grandma, my dad. All of us.'

'Sam, please, I need to know what's going on.' Georgette threw back the duvet and crossed the room and switched on Adda-Leigh's computer. She kept the phone clamped to her ear. 'Tell me how you know all this.'

But Sam wasn't listening. *'Georgette. I think I may have . . . hurt somebody. He was going to kill . . . It was horrible. I panicked.'*

Georgette typed the place names Sam had mentioned into the computer. She had to do something because she didn't know how to respond to what he'd just told her.

'There's a Glamwych in North Wales. It's a little village.' She clicked on the mouse and brought up the Internet site she'd found. 'It's . . . Oh. Wait a minute. There is no Glamwych any more. It stood on land bought by the water board. Compulsory purchase. They flooded the entire valley to make a reservoir sometime in the 1960s. The same thing happened to a couple of other Welsh valleys. Glamwych is under fifty metres of water.'

Sam interrupted her. *'I have to go there. And Streaming Point, too. We need to know what they're planning. Wales first. I have to see my grandma and my dad, to make sure they're okay.'*

'Sam, don't you think you might need our help? We could –'

'No. I'll be fine. Georgette, you have to stay with Adda-Leigh . . .'

'Of course. She's coming up to York with me for a few days.' Georgette looked at Adda-Leigh. Her friend was shifting restlessly. 'We're getting the train tomorrow. But what about you? Where are you going? Will you be okay? You sound terrible.'

'Be careful . . .' Sam said something else before the

phone went dead but his last words were drowned beneath a rising tide of hissing static. Georgette thought he might have said *'Watch out for deep water.'*

TO THE HEART OF THE STORM

The desolate building sites and graffiti-covered concrete walls, the trackside backways of King's Cross flashed by outside the window. The train picked up speed and Adda-Leigh settled back in her seat. Opposite her, Georgette placed both bony elbows on the tabletop. The engine shuddered, moving over a set of points, and sent a tremor along the whole train.

They'd heard the news reports on the radio that morning. A mysterious incident at a North London mental hospital during which a dangerous inmate had escaped.

'Seems like a good time to be getting out of London if Crisp's on the loose again. What I don't understand is, why did Sam let him out?'

'I don't think he did, at least, not intentionally. But

I told you, I couldn't get much sense out of him.'

Adda-Leigh gave an anxious sigh. 'Why couldn't he just leave well alone?'

'He wants to know what's going on. He wants us all to be safe. The Order are up to something, Addy, whether you like it or not. We all have to keep our eyes open.'

While Adda-Leigh was packing that morning, Georgette had been on her friend's computer, trawling the Internet, finding out all she could about the places Sam had mentioned. She had a sheaf of printed-out sheets in her bag.

'So you reckon Sam's gone to Wales?'

Georgette nodded.

'What about the other place?'

'Streaming Point? It's on the North Yorkshire coast. The nearest village is a place called Bernardscar.'

'Is that far from where you live?'

'Not too far. Why? What are you thinking?'

'Maybe we should go out there. Spend the day. Look around. See if we can find anything out. What connects the Order with this place? Maybe even take a walk over there and . . .'

Georgette shook her head. 'There's a nuclear power station on Streaming Point. An old one. It was shut down back in the eighties, but there's still a load of nuclear waste up there. Tons of it, apparently, in storage. They don't let anyone near there these days. Besides which, Sam said he didn't want us looking into things on our own.'

Adda-Leigh pulled a face.

But when she returned from a visit to the buffet car half an hour later there was a look of triumph in her eye. She waved her mobile phone in Georgette's face.

'Look. Sam must have changed his mind. He's sent me a text. He says we're to meet him in Bernardscar tomorrow.'

'Let me see.' Georgette reached for the phone. 'Did you get the dragon logo instead of a caller's number?'

'I didn't see it. But the text was from Sam. It said so. I don't know any other Sams.'

Georgette blinked, looking hard at the display screen on the mobile.

'It's gone. The message has gone. It was there one minute, then the next it just disappeared.'

'Well, you said it does that.'

'Not quite like that.'

'What's the matter? Why shouldn't Sam have got in touch with me for a change?'

Georgette shrugged. 'You're right. He hasn't before that's all. Still, I suppose we'd better go to Bernardscar and see what he wants.'

Adda-Leigh brightened. 'Good.'

'I thought you wanted to forget about the Order. Put it all behind you.'

Adda-Leigh waved a dismissive hand. She leaned back in her seat and looked out of the window. 'I'm tired of leaving everything to Sam.'

The train sped past a bleak industrial estate, all breezeblock and corrugated steel. Raindrops began to crosshatch the carriage windows. Soon they could see nothing but diagonal slashes snaking en masse down the surface of the glass. The train hurtled on into the heart of the storm.

Far to the west, in a sealed, windowless room with a dripping ceiling, Sister Ironspeare held a phone to her ear. The phone was connected to a computer.

'So Crisp has failed us, and yet he lives. Unfinished business, Major. But don't worry. There'll be time enough, later. For now, a change of plan is in order. The boy-dragon has a foolish habit of patching himself into the mobile phone network. Tracking was so simple. And now, using an act of imitation I have arranged for some of the mutant's friends to travel to our target zone tomorrow. If that freak of a dragon arrives too, that'll be a bonus. No, I'm not worried. He is a brute beast, he won't hinder our operations. On the contrary, Major, it will give us an opportunity to complete the first purpose of the Order, the eradication of the dragon-folk. I am confident that the Book of the Last will then confirm our glorious future. How wonderful to fulfil the first part of our destiny and learn of the next, all in one day.'

Sister Ironspeare tapped her fingertips lightly on the computer table while she listened to the major.

'No, I'm not expecting them to do anything. Neither the two girls nor their mutant companion, if he even dares to show his face amidst the chaos we've got planned. All they're going to do . . .' She paused and her thin lips twitched briefly into a smile. '. . . is die!'

The North-East London Gazette

MARSH MAN MOVED

The Marshside bog man is to be moved to the laboratories of the North-East London University, in Docklands. A team of experts from the university have been studying the body on site since its discovery. They plan to subject the corpse to minute examination. 'We hope to discover everything we can from this find,' a university spokesperson said. 'Everything from what his role was in the society he came from, to what he ate for his last meal. We are particularly excited, since no human remains of this age and in this state of preservation have ever been found in the region.'

The prehistoric youth may have been the victim of a grisly ritual of human sacrifice, as was sometimes practised in Iron Age Britain. The Museum of London plan to put the remains of the marsh man on public display when all the examinations have been completed.

Thousands of years dead, the youth from the marshes lies in a vat of preserving liquid. A team of experts in white coats intend to haul him from the safety of the chemical vat, like a baby born by Caesarean section. Then the light of day will touch his ancient skin again. But for now, deep in oblivion, he sleeps on, undisturbed.

II

Eye of the Storm

INTO THE WORLD

One Year Earlier
Luhngdou Island, South China Sea

The old man hadn't seen daylight for many years. But he knew Fen had never seen it. She'd been lowered into the cavern through a small fissure in the rock before the sun rose on the day of her birth. The hole in the rock had been sealed immediately and the old man had carried the child deep into the ground, passing through a succession of doorways hewn from solid rock, each one a little lower and a little narrower than the last, and all of which she had long since grown too large to pass through. There was no other way out. Simply by growing up, she had imprisoned herself under the ground.

The old man's flock of blind albino goats had provided the baby with an adequate substitute for mother's milk. The many miles of stone passageways had been her only home for the full fourteen years of her existence. Now she'd made a decision.

'I'm leaving,' she told the old man. *'And there's nothing you can do to stop me.'*

The manner of her leaving had convinced him his final hour had come. It was not just the wild violence with which Fen had dug her way to the surface, tearing at the stone doorways with her clawed hands, biting at the rock, worrying the dry earth, shrugging off the collapsing roof as if it were no more able to stop her than the trembling hand of the old man himself. Her manic tunnelling had forced him to shelter in the deepest recess of the devastated cave system, where what little air remained was now filled with choking dust. But worse than the total disregard she showed for his safety, worse than her contempt when he'd begged her to stay, worse than all of this, was the screaming.

As she dug, Fen had screamed, over and over again. The sound was so terrible, so filled with mindless fury and violent panic that the old man was left in no doubt. Fen was insane. Her early life below ground coupled with the transformation she had undergone in the last year, had combined to cause her already brittle personality to splinter. While she'd changed from girl to dragon, the old man had lain sick and close to death, unable to help, unable to explain. She had been altered in more ways than one. What had emerged from the ruins of her former self was truly terrifying.

And so it was that Fen left the caverns.

The old man lay face down, shivering with terror. The child he'd brought up, that he looked upon almost as a daughter, had gone.

At last, he forced himself to rise. Coughing violently, he began to feel his way across the rubble-strewn ground. He had to follow. Even if he, too, had to dig his way out with his bare hands, then he would have to try. Fen had burst out into the world. The old man didn't know who he was more afraid for.

DANCING QUEEN

Grandma Evans looked tired and very old. It was close to a year since Sam had last seen her. The strain of caring for her son, Llew Evans, Sam's father, had clearly taken its toll. Her large, solid frame had a deflated look to it, and she walked with a creaking stiffness, as if every step she took were an effort of will, a battle of mind over matter.

Sam could imagine what the last year had been like. Wheelchair-bound since the accident that ended his fire-fighting career, his father was an angry man, unable to cope with the double blow of losing his mobility and losing his wife to heart failure when she was still in her mid-thirties. Bouts of heavy drinking and a self-destructive attitude meant that Llew Evans had always been another accident waiting to happen.

When his luck ran out at last it was Sam who'd saved his life. But by that time, Sam's whole existence had altered completely and for ever.

The dragon-boy was hidden behind the greenhouse at the end of the garden. He peered at his grandmother through the streaked and dirty glass.

Sam kept perfectly still. Grandma Evans couldn't see him. He listened to her wheezing breath and her disjointed snatches of song. She was hanging washing on the line, near the back door of her stone-walled house. The skies had cleared and the winter sunshine lit up the garden with its scrubby vegetable patch and flower beds. The dark-green leaves of daffodil plants were pushing up through the earth like fingertips, feeling the air for any signs of spring.

Sam didn't know his grandmother all that well. It was something he regretted. There'd been a falling out between her and Llew, which only his recent life-threatening accident had brought to an end. For much of Sam's life they'd seen very little of the old woman. He and Llew had lived in London. Grandma Evans lived in Wales. There had been no visiting, in either direction.

Hearing her voice, he imagined she might be singing in Welsh, a traditional ballad perhaps. But he listened closer and recognised the song. 'Dancing Queen' by Abba.

'Lah dah dah, only seventeen.' Grandma Evans sang with a wooden clothes peg gripped between her teeth. She attached a man's shirt to the line and turned away. The shirt billowed in the wind.

Sam closed his eyes. He reached out with his mind, carefully, slowly. He didn't want to startle the old woman, or frighten her. He didn't want to show himself. How could he let her see him, as he was now? But still, he had to speak to her.

'Grandma.' From inside his head his voice sounded just as it had, back before the transformation had made ordinary speech a thing of the past. Sam let the calling of the name form in his mind. Silently, he sounded out the word. Then at last, he released it, feeling it settle into his grandmother's consciousness.

Her head snapped back. She turned, slowly, rotating her thick waist, scanning the garden.

'Sam?' There was a catch in Grandma Evans's voice. 'Where are you?'

'I'm here.' His mind-voice sounded small and lost, like a child abandoned in some endless wilderness, calling out with no hope of any reply. But Grandma Evans could hear him and she'd recognised his voice.

'Come out, Sammy.' Her voice was textured by age, but still soft with kindness. 'Come on out. I won't hurt you, love. You're safe here. Didn't I tell you, you'd always be welcome?'

She knew how he'd changed. She would understand, wouldn't she?

Sam closed his eyes and let all his senses search the area around his grandmother's garden. There was no one around, no neighbours, no passers-by, not even a dog or a cat to witness this unusual family reunion. So he lifted a clawed hand and gripped the wooden frame of the greenhouse. He bent back his head, scaly muzzle pointed skywards. He spread his toes, digging at the earth, and he tried to stand up. The coiled tangle of his tail prevented it. He let out a moan of effort. A plume of white smoke shot from one nostril. If he could just stand on two legs, like a human being, perhaps then he wouldn't look so monstrous.

He could have spread his wings, beat the air, and hung with his feet trailing just above the ground. That he knew he could manage. But the wings weren't human. They were terrible things, made of stretched and scaly skin pulled tight over mutated muscle, bone and sinew. He wouldn't use his wings. He wanted to stand up straight and let his grandmother look at him. He didn't want to give her a heart attack.

His toes buckled and twisted under his own weight. His feet bent back agonisingly, but he managed to straighten his backbone, keeping his wings carefully folded out of sight. He stood swaying, towering above the greenhouse roof, and looked towards the house.

The washing basket was on the lawn. Half the wash swung on the drooping line. Grandma Evans wasn't there.

She was behind him. She'd skirted around the greenhouse while he'd been putting all his efforts into standing upright. So much for telepathic powers. He turned. The old woman looked up at him.

'Hello, Sammy,' she said. 'You've grown.'

There was real warmth in her eyes. Sam felt a terrible ache. He'd lived like an orphan for too long.

'*Grandma. I have to warn you. It's the Order, they —*'

Sam broke off. Something was wrong. He sensed the danger now, and his instincts screamed at him to drop on to all fours or soar into the sky and escape. He couldn't fade into invisibility, not while his forced posture was causing him so much pain. Still, he couldn't bear to break the old woman's gaze. He couldn't become a beast again, in front of her. She looked at him as if she'd known him all her life.

And so he listened as the window in the upstairs back bedroom of the cottage swung open. He heard a quick breath taken in, and a finger pressed to the trigger of a gun. He heard the twin shells hurtling from the barrels of the shotgun and felt the pellets slam into his skin, burning and lacerating.

He fell sideways, smashing through glass and wood, collapsing into the old greenhouse and bringing a great chaos of pain and misery piling on top of him. Pain, from the gunshot wounds and the deep cuts from shards of glass. And misery, because he knew who it was that had shot him.

RIVER DOG

They stood on the bridge and watched the river for a while. The city of York was spread out on either side of them. It would be dark soon.

'There's a local train that runs all the way to Bernardscar,' Georgette said.

'A nice trip to the seaside.' Adda-Leigh grinned. 'I should've brought my bikini. Mind you, I wouldn't fancy a swim in *that*!' She nodded at the river. Georgette looked down at the water swirling under the bridge. The River Ouse was horribly swollen, its waters barely contained by either bank. Rain dimpled its seething surface. Pools and puddles had collected on the towpath that ran alongside.

'Looks like it'd drag you down and roll you around and spit you out again ten miles down river when you were good and dead.'

Georgette smiled. She felt the rain patting her on the top of her head. Her hair was soaked, hanging in rat-tails around her face. Adda-Leigh, just as bedraggled, grinned back.

'There might be a flood,' Georgette said.

'Ye deluge!'

'I'm serious. York floods all the time. There's a pub on the river that holds canoe races around the bar whenever the Ouse breaks its banks.'

'You're joking! We'll have to go there!'

'Don't be daft. They'd throw us out.'

'Why would they?'

'Because we're both fifteen! You might pass for eighteen, I suppose, but you know I look about twelve!'

Adda-Leigh smiled. 'Oh, come on. Let's find a cafe or something.' She took Georgette by the arm. 'I'm wet and I'm cold. I might as well be drowning!'

'We'll all be drowning if this rain keeps up!'

'That's right, girl. It's the end of the world as we know it.'

Georgette looked at her friend. 'We should build an ark.'

Adda-Leigh grinned and shook her head. They set off over the bridge and down along the rainswept pavement.

'I'll have to phone Aaron later,' Georgette said. 'I

emailed him, but I don't know if he read it. I need to tell him what Sam said, about all of us being in danger.'

'He won't listen. The boy's a fool.'

'Yeah. But that's better than being a dead fool. I'll just tell him to keep his eyes open.'

Behind them the river swept on, straining at its banks like a great muscular dog, pulling at its leash, hungry to come spilling over the sides, eager to make the land its own.

CHEESE BEAN SPECIAL

Aaron was in the kitchen, making a cheese bean special. With his mobile clamped to his face as he worked, he talked Georgette through the process.

'First, you open up a tin of beans. Then you get your digestive biscuit. Bung it on the grill, like so.'

Georgette tried to interrupt. 'Aaron . . .'

'Then you get a spoon.' Aaron rummaged through the cutlery piled up on the drainer by the sink. 'And you ladle some beans on to your biscuit. Like . . . so!'

'Aaron, listen . . .'

'And then, the crowning glory, so to speak. The cheese.' Aaron opened the fridge and peered inside. He pushed a box of eggs aside, lifted a soggy plastic bag containing a limp, brown-edged lettuce, and underneath he found half a pack of mild Cheddar wrapped in cellophane, oily to the touch.

'Aaron, listen to me . . .'

Aaron grabbed the cheese and shut the fridge door. He snatched a knife off the drainer.

'Aaron, I . . .'

'You slice a bit of cheese, nice and thick.'

'Aaron! Will you shut up a minute?'

Aaron was silent.

'Thank you.'

He sighed deeply. 'I got your email, George. I heard about that business up at Stoneberry. I know you and Sam think we're in danger and all that. I thought you'd appreciate a cookery lesson. I was just trying to take your mind off everything.' Delicately, Aaron bit the edge of the sliced cheese with his front teeth, expertly reshaping it, from rectangle to circle. 'Plus, of course, I haven't had my tea yet.'

Georgette snorted. 'Sounds like you've made a good start.'

Aaron returned to the grill pan and carefully positioned the circle of cheese over the bean-topped biscuit. He threw the knife into the washing-up bowl. 'Thing is, George, I just don't believe we're in as much trouble as you seem to think we are. I mean the police . . .'

'The police! Aaron, don't be an idiot! The police

don't know anything about the Order! Imagine trying to explain it to them? Oh yes, officer, there's this ancient order of secret knights that want to kill us. Oh yes, and normally they kill dragons. Did you know Crisp was hanging around near St Michael's the other day, before he got arrested?'

'Yes. And now he's escaped. The police'll catch him. They know who he is, George. They'll get him.'

Aaron found a matchbox amongst the crumbs around the breadboard. He shook the box, to see if it was full, pulled out a match and lit the gas over the grill.

'Come on, George, you worry too much! Sometimes I think all that business last summer was just a bad dream. I know Sam's gone, but maybe he did just run off to live in a squat somewhere. Okay, so I've seen things. Really peculiar things. But it's all so weird! It's hard to believe it. I mean, how can an ordinary kid like Sam turn into a dragon? It's just not possible!'

Georgette made an exasperated squeak. 'Aaron! You saw him yourself!'

Aaron laughed. 'You sound like a mouse with hiccups!'

Georgette's tone remained grave. 'We're in danger, Aaron. I don't care what you say. I'm keeping you informed. It's for your own safety. Just take a moment to think about it. You need to open your eyes.'

Aaron stopped laughing and gave a sudden gasp. 'Oh no!'

'I'm glad you've decided to take things seriously at last.' Georgette's voice had a self-righteous ring to it, but Aaron was no longer listening.

The mobile slipped to the lino-covered floor. Aaron lunged at the cooker and yanked the grill pan back. He beat at the flaming biscuit with a tea towel he'd hastily snatched from the work surface. 'George! You made me burn my cheese bean special!'

By the time he picked up his phone again Georgette had hung up.

THE TRAP

Nine months earlier
Russia

The trapper looked at the dead wolf. It was clear from the expression in his eyes, blinking beneath his fur hat, that the man didn't understand how the creature had died. The trap held it firm by the front leg. But something had torn its head off.

The forest was still. Everything fell quiet when she was around. The birds, the animals, the insects. They knew what she was.

Fen watched from the cover of the pines as the trapper knelt in the bloody snow and wrinkled his forehead, looking at the tracks she'd deliberately left behind. She couldn't help but laugh out loud at the look on his face as he gazed fearfully around him at the silent forest. She was playing.

Fen could still laugh, though the noise she made didn't sound much like an expression of mirth. It was a tortured sound. A laugh that boiled and hissed from the back of her throat, over rows of teeth, exploding into the air in a maniacal scream. The noise reverberated through the forest. When she saw the effect it had on the lone trapper, Fen laughed again.

For a brief second she remembered another time, years before. Her laughter had sounded different then, when she was younger, when she was a little girl. A little girl growing up in an underground cavern with Qua, the old man, her guardian and only companion. He'd been telling her stories. About dragons. And she'd laughed because she was afraid.

She'd been able to tell, even then, before the changes came on her, that there was something not quite right about this laughter. Qua had creased his brow, puzzled and a little alarmed. He couldn't understand why she was laughing.

But now, remembering the old man just made her angry. She flexed her wings, spreading them above her shoulders, shaking the snow off in a jerky trembling. Qua had held back the truth, betrayed her from the moment she was born. He'd tried to convince her to stay with him, buried beneath the ground for ever.

And he'd never told her what she really was. When the transformation started, of course, he hadn't been able to keep his secret any longer.

Fen beat her wings, giving her the lift she needed to scuttle up the trunk of the pine tree, her clawed hands ripping at the bark as she climbed. She knew the trapper was running. She could sense his desperate fear, his blundering and panic-stricken progress through the snow-choked wood. She didn't have to see him to know exactly where he was. His stench was thick in the air, his rasping breath and pounding heart echoed in her head, hurting her, smothering her thoughts with his unwanted presence.

She followed, gliding just above the snow-topped pines, her trailing tail dislodging little avalanches to let her quarry know she was coming. At last, when she could bear his presence no longer, just as he reached the place where the trees thinned out close to the edge of the forest, she fell. Like a booted foot descending to crush a centipede. She fell to earth, and stamped out another little life.

THE HEALING OF WOUNDS

Pieces of broken glass were everywhere. Sam lay amid the ruin of the greenhouse and stared up at the sky. Rainclouds had gathered and the brief spell of sunshine had been smothered out.

His head was crowned with broken terracotta and spilled compost. Plant bulbs trailed their pallid and spindly roots about his scaly cranium. Sam's wings were twisted painfully under his back, his tail coiled beneath a fallen trestle table. There was an agonising throbbing in his side. He felt his healing flesh pushing at the shotgun pellets, forcing the fragments back out through the already closing wounds. He felt sick with pain. A terrible heat, then an intense cold swept through his body. Sam shook his head and bit down hard on his tongue and spat out a plume of blood-flecked ashes. He couldn't hide. He couldn't lie still. The pain was too great. He lay exposed.

Somewhere beyond the fringe of his agony, he was aware of the sounds. His hearing focused on the stair lift, operating inside the house. Then the turning of the wheels. The wheelchair moving over the concrete slabs of the garden path. But even without these clues he still would have known who was coming.

It was Llew. It was his father. The man who'd brought him up, from the day Sam's mother died to the day the dragon-boy had left home. His dad. The man who'd just shot him.

Grandma Evans spoke, her voice low and hoarse with shock. 'What have you done?'

'Mam.' Llew barely whispered the word. 'What is it? That thing . . .'

'You know who it is!'

Sam heard the wheelchair roll forward, crunching on broken glass.

'You've known all along! How could you shoot at him! Your own boy!'

'But Mam . . .' Llew was close now. Sam could feel his father's gaze falling on him. He couldn't look at the man. 'This can't be him.' Llew's voice was thick with a helpless misery. 'It just can't be!'

'Hush.' Grandma Evans raised her voice a little. 'Don't listen to your dad, Sammy. He may be able to swim thirty lengths a day, legs or no legs, but he's still as daft as a brush. I've told him about you, over and over, but he doesn't listen. Cloth ears, that's his problem. Always has been.'

Sam shivered. A great trembling took hold of him. He gasped. A tray full of seed potatoes, dislodged from a sagging shelf, fell on his chest, bouncing off his scaly skin. He hadn't heard his father's voice for almost a year.

'Is he . . .?' The man in the wheelchair took a sharp breath. 'Is he badly hurt?'

'Speak to the boy, for heaven's sake, Llewellyn! Ask him yourself.'

There was a long silence. Sam looked at the sky. The cloud cover had thickened. The daylight grew very dim.

'I thought . . .' Llew swallowed hard. 'When I looked out and saw you there with Mam . . .' He struggled for breath, as if, like Sam, he were in pain. 'When I saw you I was scared,' he said at last. He breathed a little easier then. 'I just saw a threat. Something big and frightening. And so I got the gun. We keep it for foxes and that. Always bothering the hens, they are. And what with the way you look, I thought . . .' Llew coughed, awkwardly.

Sam lifted his head. Loose compost and splinters of glass slid off his spine-covered scalp as he rose from the debris. He looked at his father. There was Llew, sitting in his new lightweight wheelchair, a human being, a man of flesh and blood, of muscle and bone. Sam could tell his father had stopped drinking alcohol and that the burns he'd received in the fire a year ago had almost healed. He could sense the man's vigorous health and strength. Apart from the old spinal injury, damage too severe ever to be treated, Sam thought Llew looked stronger and fitter than he'd ever known him.

And yet at the same time he'd never seemed weaker or more vulnerable. He'd shaved off his habitual moustache. This made him look younger than Sam remembered. But his black hair had turned to silver at the temples. The contrast was unsettling.

Llew coughed. He wouldn't look at Sam.

The dragon-boy lay back down in the dirt and the broken glass. The shotgun wounds in his side were healing fast, but still his domed forehead burned with a feverish heat.

Grandma Evans whispered to the man in the wheelchair, but Sam could hear every word. 'Has it really come to this? Did you have to try to kill your own son, before you'd believe in him?' She sounded weary.

'How bad is he? I don't see any blood.'

The old woman took a moment before she replied. 'Some hurts go beyond healing.'

Then the rain came down, a sudden, hard shower, falling in ice-cold droplets that hissed and spat, rising again as steam from Sam's burning brow.

CREST OF THE RIDGE

Rensall, Paxton Wyke, Nortby. The stations and halts rolled by. And in between there were fields and farmland, rough pasture and forest. There were farmhouses, with raindrops bouncing off their slate roofs. Woods bare of leaf, the trees black against the sky. Half a dozen crows, flapping over the carcass of a drowned sheep in a flooded ditch. Rain.

The electric train was two carriages long. It was going to take them three hours to get to Bernardscar. They'd set out early. Very early.

Adda-Leigh yawned and shifted in her seat. 'God, how much longer! These seats are killing me!'

'Two more stops,' said Georgette. 'Knapper and Werby. Then we'll be there.'

Adda-Leigh turned to the window. 'Talk about filthy

weather . . .' She gazed out at the dismal scenery. They were passing a bleak hillside, one small stranded outpost of the Yorkshire Moors that lay further to the north. An outcrop of exposed rock jutted from the crest of the ridge. A lone figure was standing on the outcrop.

Adda-Leigh pressed her face to the rain-streaked carriage window.

'Georgette. Look. There's someone out there.'

'Probably just some farmer.'

'No look. It's a woman. Up on the top of that rock. What's she doing? We're in the middle of nowhere.'

'Could be a rambler. One of those mad outdoor types.'

But Adda-Leigh continued to stare out of the window, long after the train had swept past the hill and down to the scattered farmsteads of Knapper. The figure on the rocky outcrop hadn't looked like a farmer or a rambler. She hadn't looked like anyone who should be out on a rainswept hillside in February. A small woman. Long black hair. She wasn't even wearing a coat.

The woman was watching the train. And Adda-Leigh had the distinct impression, even though the distance made it impossible for her to have actually seen it, that the woman had looked into the carriage. She'd picked out the very spot where Adda-Leigh was sitting, and had gazed deep into her eyes.

UN(HAN(IN(WORLD

In the high-tech preserving vat, the youth's body remains unchanged. Electronics hum, a steady temperature is maintained. The corpse is safe here. Just as safe as it was below the ground, in the protective earth of the marshes.

And it hasn't been moved very far. Just a few kilometres. Out across the marsh, along the canal to the Thames, then following the twists of the river to where the docks once operated. Here, in the brand-new historical research buildings of the University of North-East London, the body has found a new resting place.

The great metropolis would be a marvel to the dead youth, if he could somehow be made aware of his surroundings. And the university laboratories would be a place of terror and wonder to him. And yet the wetlands and the river, the reeds and the harsh stench of the dark water, the damp air of Marshside just a short distance away, all this would have been familiar.

But he sees and hears nothing. He is as cold and lifeless as stone.

The laboratory bides its time. The university awaits the arrival of experts from Sweden and from Ireland. Applications for grant funding are submitted. The pace of academic research is slow. But there's no rush. The boy in the preserving vat is going nowhere.

THE LODGER

The doorbell rang while Aaron and his family were sitting in the living room, watching the television and eating their tea. Fried egg and oven chips, sliced tomatoes and frozen peas. Aaron had polished off his meal before anyone else, with the plate balanced on his knees and the hot china warming him through his jeans. Now he was eyeing his younger sister's plate, forking up the odd chip that had strayed too far from the rest and gobbling it down while Dawn's round eyes were held firmly by the flickering TV set.

'Get the door, Aaron.'

'Oh, Mum! Can't Dawn go?'

'I brought the drink in,' Dawn said. An empty plastic Coke bottle lay on the carpet in front of them. Dawn tapped it with her foot. 'Besides, Aaron keeps stealing my chips.'

Aaron let out a long-suffering sigh and shook his head.

'Okay, okay! I'll go. You're so childish.'

Dawn smiled happily. 'Am not.'

'Am!'

The doorbell rang again.

'Aaron! You heard your mother! Now . . . go . . . and . . . get . . . the . . . door!' Aaron's father uttered each syllable separately, for special emphasis.

Aaron dragged himself up off the couch and stomped out of the room, making sure he nudged Dawn's plate with his knee as he went past.

'Hoi!'

Grinning with pleasure at this small, undeserved victory, and still holding his fork in one hand, Aaron opened the door.

The old man stood on the doorstep. He was dressed in worn, pale-coloured robes. Nut-brown skin, Oriental features, his ancient face was the texture of cracked leather. There was a thin cord around his neck, from which dangled a pendant fashioned from a short length of bamboo. Aaron could only stare dumbly. What could this bizarre-looking man want with them?

The old man smiled and walked straight into the house. Stick thin, he easily had room to slip past and down the hall, the faded robes billowing around his emaciated form.

'Mum! Dad!' Aaron called, his voice high-pitched with alarm. 'There's a man!'

But the old man was already in the living room. Aaron heard Dawn's squeal of surprise. He trailed after the man, not knowing what else to do, but he left the front door open, in case they had to forcibly eject their unexpected visitor.

Aaron peered around the door in time to see the look of bemused astonishment on his parents' faces as the old man bowed before them.

'You will forgive my intrusion.' His English was perfect. He smiled. 'I have come about the room.'

'The room? Yes, of course. I was thinking about the room only this morning. How we ought to rent it out.' Aaron's father stood up, his empty dinner plate in one hand.

Aaron's mother also got to her feet. 'I thought I'd contact that agency on the high street,' she said.

'Of course. It was they who sent me.'

'But I haven't phoned them yet. Or have I?' Aaron could hear the doubt in his mother's voice.

The old man was unperturbed. 'I have one month's rental money. Here. In advance.' He delved into his robes and emerged with a wad of twenty-pound notes clutched awkwardly in his fist. 'I am very pleased with this location, so I offer you an extra ten pounds per week. You will accept.'

Still the man smiled. But while the smile implied that he had just made a polite enquiry, his tone had been more like a statement of fact.

'Well . . . er . . . okay!' Aaron's father laughed awkwardly. 'You seem to have made us an offer we can't refuse! Mister . . . er . . .'

'Qua.'

'Mister . . . er . . . Qua. Welcome to our home.'

But Aaron wasn't listening to his father's silly laughter and dithering speech. He could hardly believe what had just taken place. No one had mentioned anything about renting out the spare room. The idea seemed to have appeared from nowhere, to have blown into his parents' heads just as Qua himself had breezed into the house.

Aaron looked at the old man, standing with his hands laid palm to palm in front of his chest having just passed over the rent money. From the deep scarring of the twisted fingers and damaged joints it was clear these hands had been put through some terrible trauma. Whether the wounds were self-inflicted or the work of another was impossible to tell. But to Aaron they looked like hands that had been beaten with a hammer.

MIND INVADER

Three months earlier
Arctic Sea

Fen pushed through the freezing water, swimming amongst a slush of ice fragments, keeping just below the surface swell. The heave and pull of the ocean pulsed within her mind like an abstract thought. But still she couldn't forget about the old man, even though she'd not set eyes on him for months now.

She'd left him under the earth, but she knew he wasn't dead. She had killed the goats. They'd seemed to expect it, turning their blind eyes upon her, their habitual bleating replaced by a strange, shifting silence. The old man, however, had cried out. He'd begged and pleaded. But not for his life. He had wanted her to stay in the catacombs for ever, wanted her to stay imprisoned for all eternity, and that she could not forgive.

All her life she'd been a prisoner and Qua had been her jailer. She hadn't even known it. Not until the transformation had come over her. Then, when she invaded the old man's mind, plundered his memories and rifled through his tattered dreams, she'd found the truth at last. And now, even here, in the wide, bleak emptiness of this northern sea, she couldn't forget what they'd done to her.

FATHER TO SON

'Come into the house, Sammy.'

Sam had lain a day and a night without moving, amidst the ruins of his grandmother's greenhouse. Each time he closed his eyes, the image of Adda-Leigh, drowning, had filled his mind, tormenting him with anxiety. He'd forced himself to block it out. He lay sleepless, staring up at the clouds that boiled by overhead, waiting for his body to repair itself.

The shotgun wounds had healed at last. Just the scars remained, fresher than the many other reminders of old hurts that covered his pitted body.

He thought of his father, and the fire at the Marshside flat they'd lived in, which had nearly ended Llew's life. The chip pan in flames. The whisky bottle. His father in a drunken stupor. Sam's flight across the marsh, when he was still in the first throes of his terrible metamorphosis, rushing to the rescue. It was all seared into his memory for ever.

'Sam. Sammy. Come inside.' Grandma Evans spoke out loud. She was sitting at the kitchen table. Sam, lying outside with his body pressed against the cottage wall, could hear her old heart beating steadily inside her ribcage. She wasn't afraid of him. He could sense her trust, as well as her poignant longing for all the rifts in her family to be healed. But he knew how remote that possibility was, and he knew that he was to blame.

He'd done what he came to do. He'd warned his grandma about the threat posed by the Order while he lay recuperating in the shattered greenhouse. He'd seen with his own eyes that nothing suspicious was going on. There was no sign of any immediate danger. Now his gunshot wounds had healed. He was stronger than ever before. He ought to leave, to follow up his mission to investigate the Order's new leader, at her HQ, here in Wales. But something was holding him back, if only for a while. He wanted to be with his family.

'Come on in now, Sammy love. It'll be all right, see.'

But Llew was also in the kitchen, sitting in his wheelchair by the stove. His hands gripped the wheels, as if to make ready for sudden flight. His heart was pounding out an anxious tattoo. His breathing was tight and jerky. Sam knew his father was terrified of him.

In the year since he'd last seen Llew, Sam's psychic abilities had grown stronger and had developed, at an instinctive level. Now he found his father's presence was enough to unearth a maelstrom of buried memories, both Llew's and his own. Memories that had churned beneath the surface of their lives together since the day he was born. He saw his father in a new light. Not just the embittered paraplegic, the angry Welshman living in the heart of a despised England. Not just the dysfunctional father he'd lived with in the flat in Marshside, but also the young fireman, defying the disapproval of his brothers and colleagues alike when he married a young Oriental girl he'd rescued from a blazing Chinese restaurant. He saw too, his father's battle to regain his health over the past twelve months, after the terrible burns he'd suffered, and from the years of alcohol abuse that had preceded the accident. He saw all his strength, and the wild freedom of spirit that had captured his mother's heart. And now, seeing all this for the first time, Llew's horror at what Sam had become cut him deeper than he would have thought possible.

'Do you like cake? I've made cake. Come on in, love. Please.'

Sam didn't want to enter the kitchen. He ached to remain hidden, out of sight. His grandmother lived in the last house on the street. Her only neighbour was out at work. There was just Grandma Evans and his father there to see him. And yet he hesitated. His scaled skin crawled at the thought of his father's eyes upon him. But there was a part of him that desperately wanted to claim at least some fragment of his old life back. He couldn't stop himself crawling towards the door. His granny was calling him in from the garden. The pull of his lost childhood was irresistible. She'd made a cake.

Sam extended a single claw and gently pushed the door open. Silence from inside the house. Two hearts beat in the kitchen. Two pairs of eyes waited to watch him come in. He swallowed the fiery bile that had gathered in his throat and slithered forward. Still hugging the wall, he rounded the doorjamb and crossed the threshold. The worn stone step was cool and smooth against his belly.

'That's it, Sammy. Here, sit at the table.'

Grandma Evans gestured to a wooden chair pulled back from the rough-hewn kitchen table. The warm scent of baking, rich and sweet and all pervading, filled the room. Sam's head swam. He slipped across the floor, his claws clicking on the flagstones. He clambered on to the chair, his long stomach resting against the wooden seat, his tail stretched over the flags to keep his balance. He rose, swaying over the table. The spines of his crest brushed the beams of the ceiling. He didn't dare look at Llew. Desperately, he blocked out all sense of what his father was thinking.

Grandma Evans looked up at him. She brushed at her eyes with the back of her large, weather-beaten hand.

'Have a piece of cake, Sammy.'

It had been months since Sam had eaten anything. He was never hungry any more and didn't seem to need food at all. But still he bent his long neck and reached down to the plate on the table in front of him, on which a slice of crumbly yellow Madeira cake lay. Carefully, he lowered his muzzle towards the cake, stretched out his lips and coiled his tongue around the slice. He closed his eyes and took it into his mouth. The cake seemed to melt like a sugary snowflake. Sam felt it dissolving into his blood and running through his arteries like milk and honey.

And then he heard the squeak of the wheels, the chair hissing across the flagstones, the hands jerkily pushing at the tyres.

'I'm sorry but I can't! I just can't!' Llew was bellowing at the top of his voice. Sam opened his eyes to see his grandmother's face, full of hurt surprise.

'This is too much! You might be able to sit here and

watch that thing eat cake at the kitchen table, but I can't! I don't care, even if it is my Sam, I shall be sick I tell you!'

The wheelchair scraped against the doorframe as Llew rolled himself into the hall. Sam sprang backwards, the wooden chair he'd been leaning on went somersaulting over the flagstones, the table scraped and clattered as he pushed against it. He hurled himself headfirst out through the kitchen door, his wings tightly folded. He couldn't stop a flicker of flame bursting from between his lips and scorching the lintel as he passed.

'Sammy!' Grandma Evans called after him, but he wasn't listening. He twisted in the air, corkscrewing low across the garden, then opened his wings and shot upwards into the falling rain and darkening sky. Tears burst from his eyes in a shower of blue sparks and his howl of anguish, wrapped in the wind and rattle of the storm, set the dogs barking all along the valley.

His father's words rang in his ears, *even if it is my Sam . . . even if it is . . .*

TEA CEREMONY

'Please come in.' Aaron heard the old man call out from behind the door of the spare room. 'Simply push the door. It will open.'

Aaron still thought of it as the spare room but it wasn't spare any more. It was where the lodger lived. It was Qua's room.

Aaron still couldn't quite believe it. His family had never been a sociable lot when it came to entertaining at home. Both parents and children treated the few, brief visits from relatives at Christmas or on birthdays as a tedious duty, something to be endured rather than enjoyed. Neither Aaron nor Dawn was much inclined to invite friends around, usually offering the excuse that their house was too boring a place to hang out. But the truth was, the family were never happier than when it was just the four of them slouched in front of the television, passing round the baked potatoes and the spicy chicken wings.

And yet now, out of the blue, an old Chinese man had turned up at the house and Aaron's parents had suddenly announced that they were looking for a lodger. Before you knew it there he was, living in their midst as if he were the fifth member of the family.

Except, Aaron had to admit, it wasn't really anything like that. He was living with them, yes, but not as one of the family. Qua kept to his room most of the time. He cooked and ate his own meals there. He never went out. Aaron hadn't even seen him in the kitchen or the garden.

In fact, Aaron had hardly seen the old man at all. And that was why it was with a feeling of some trepidation that he pushed open the door and went into what had once been the spare room. Qua was still an unknown quantity.

Aaron had been expecting the old man's room to smell strongly of unfamiliar food, something harsh and heavily spiced. A small electric cooker with a single ring stood on the floor in the corner of the room. On top of the cooker, a thin broth was simmering in a battered wok. But the air beyond the door barely held any aroma at all.

The room was unrecognisable. A hammock had

been slung in one corner. A round rug, patterned in faded blue and orange and frayed at the edges, had been placed in the middle of the floor. A red paper lantern shaded the light bulb that hung from the ceiling, but the walls were bare and the room had been cleared of all furniture.

Qua himself was sitting on the rug, his thin legs folded under him. He smiled at Aaron and spread one of his ruined hands in a gesture of welcome. With his other hand he played thoughtfully with the bamboo pendant he always wore around his neck.

'Sit,' he said.

'Mum thought you might like some tea.' Aaron held out the mug a little too quickly. The milky brew slopped against the side and a line of drips pattered down on to the rug. The old man's smile didn't waver.

Aaron's mum had been filled with anxious guilt since Qua had announced he would be cooking for himself. The rent she'd taken from the old man was generous. She felt she should be providing his meals. The offer of tea was a rather poor attempt to compensate, and Aaron had been bribed into delivering the mug with an offer of an evening off the family washing-up rota.

'Please,' Qua said. 'Sit.'

Aaron knelt down. There was a china teapot with a wicker handle steaming gently on the rug. A small jade-green cup had been placed beside it. Aaron looked at the tea in the mug in his hand, doubtfully. Tan blotches, like the blemishes on the back of an old person's hand, spotted the surface. He pushed the drink towards Qua.

'Many thanks,' the old man said. 'You will accept a cup in return.'

Aaron coughed. He hadn't wanted to stay, but he felt too embarrassed to simply turn around and leave. He shrugged.

'Sure. Why not. Cheers.'

Qua picked up his teapot by its wicker handle, lifted it high and poured a stream of pale golden liquid into the little green cup without spilling a drop. He then placed the cup in front of Aaron in a manner reminiscent of a chess master moving a piece and putting his opponent in checkmate.

Qua raised the mug Aaron had brought him. It was printed with the words I LOVE MY CUPPA. The old man lifted it to his lips and drank. His smile became a little fixed.

'I wasn't sure about the sugar,' Aaron said, 'so I only gave you three spoons.' Now Aaron lifted the jade green cup, gripping the rim, having looked in vain for a handle. He sniffed at the tea the old man had poured him and then took a small sip. The drink was hot and strong and tasted like the smell of dry grass in late summer. Aaron swallowed and put the cup down on the rug.

'Good,' said Qua. 'We have taken tea together.'

Aaron grinned and nodded, humouring the old man. He cleared his throat, mentally preparing the words he was about to say – something about having homework to get on with, and thanks for the tea, and bye-bye.

'Your homework you can leave until later,' Qua said.

Aaron stared at him, stunned.

'Wait. How did –?'

Qua smiled and held up one scarred hand, waving away the stammered question. His next words reduced Aaron to shocked silence.

'Tell me what you know of boys who turn into dragons, Aaron.'

EDGE OF SHADOW

Two days ago
Norwegian Sea

Fen lay in deep water and watched the killer whale cruising on the surface of the sea, hundreds of metres above her. She had let herself sink into near total darkness, down to the very edge of shadow, the depth beyond which sunlight cannot reach. The pressure there was immense, and yet she was untroubled by it. Her hide and bone could withstand far greater challenges. She looked up from the inky darkness, and her piercing vision had no difficulty tracking the black and white beast swimming far above her, unaware, for the moment, of her scrutiny.

It was always the predators she hunted. Wolf,

bear, killer whale, human. She slaughtered them, not to satisfy any physical hunger – like Sam, she had no need of food and hadn't eaten at all for over a year – she killed them simply because they made her feel uncomfortable. They reminded her too much of herself.

She shadowed the whale, which swam on, oblivious to her presence. But at the back of Fen's mind something was stirring. She knew now that her travels in the world of air and sunlight were not as random as they'd seemed. She'd been searching for something, instinctively moving towards it before she even knew it was there.

There was land not so very far away. A wild and jagged coastline cut with inlets and dusted with little islands and jagged rocks. She could pick out the contours of the mainland from feeling the swirl of the sea. She could already taste the rock and soil of the place, even here, in the deep water. Further inland there would be mountains and lochs, rivers and towns, then, further still, placid lowlands, regimented fields and seething cities of men.

Mentally, she followed the coast south. There was a place, a meeting point. Here, the lines would intersect. It wasn't far. Not for her. A name formed itself from somewhere within her extra-sensory perceptions. Streaming Point. She knew she would go there. She didn't know why yet, but that didn't worry her. She would find out, by and by.

This new sense of purpose cheered Fen, somehow. She gave a sudden thrash of her tail and sped through the dense water, feeling the pressure falling away as she soared up from the deep. She hit the killer whale before it was even aware of her approach and dragged it, thrashing, out of the water. She cleared the churning surface with her wings beating the air furiously, sending a halo of spray flying out all around her.

Later, as she floated amongst the torn remains of the butchered sea mammal, a cloud of gulls appeared, drawn by the scent of blood. Fen burst out of the sea once more and screamed at them, ruffling their feathers with the power of her cry as the birds scattered in terrified flight.

'Tell them!' she called out loud, her voice, slurred and distorted. The words, recognisable only to herself, carried over the empty ocean. 'Tell them on Streaming Point! Tell them Fen is on her way! Tell them death is coming!'

SCORCHED GRASS

A row of trees and a tangled bramble hedge stood between Grandma Evans's garden and the field at the back of the house. Splintered and torn branches hung from the trees and the hedge was burning. Sam was in the field, lying on his side, his body coiled, plumes of smoke streaming from his nostrils with every breath he let out.

He had fallen into a state of exhausted calm by the time his grandmother arrived. She stood over him.

'Sam,' she said. 'Sammy.'

Without thinking, Sam tried to speak. The sound he made was low and harsh and held no meaning other than as an expression of his pain. Flames flickered from his mouth, licking at the singed grass. Grandma Evans took a step back.

Sam lifted a clawed hand, his long talons spread in a gesture of helplessness. He swallowed painfully, forcing the burning pitch back down his throat. The words formed in his mind and he let them drift into his grandmother's consciousness.

'Grandma . . . I'm sorry. I'm sorry about the trees and the hedge.'

The old woman shrugged. 'The fire in the hedge will burn itself out. The trees will heal. You had to do something to let off steam, didn't you? What your father said, well it was terrible. But if you give him a bit of time I know he'll see what a fool he's being. He'll come to realise how he really feels about you, Sammy, I'm sure of it.'

'It's not Dad. Or it's not just Dad. I have to go. I've been here too long.'

'Sammy, you had to let yourself heal.'

'And if I hadn't come here I wouldn't have been wounded in the first place.'

Grandma Evans hung her head. 'I know, love. He's my son, but Llew Evans can be a terrible fool some-times.'

'It's the others, Gran. My friends. The Order said they'd kill them. And there's this girl . . .' Sam's words trailed off.

'You're worried about her?' said Grandma Evans, gently. 'Well that's understandable.'

'I didn't know what to do. Should I have stayed close to

her, in case anything happens, instead of charging off trying to find out what's going on?'

The old woman knelt down carefully in the blackened grass. 'Well, you're out to stop the Order doing anyone any harm, whichever way you go about it. And you wanted to make sure the rest of us were in no danger, too. I think you chose the braver option, Sammy. You can't be in two places at once.'

Sam lifted his muzzle and gazed up at his grandmother. *'I know that. But it's tearing me apart.'* He gave a sigh, and a small puff of smoke, like a miniature raincloud, rolled across his tongue and hung above the scorched meadow.

Grandma Evans reached out and laid a hand on Sam's scaled head.

'There,' she murmured, soothingly. 'Don't you worry, Sammy. Don't you worry.'

But they both knew there was plenty still to worry about.

DAY TRIPPERS

The downpour showed no signs of abating. Rain hammered on the corrugated tin roof that covered the platform on Bernardscar Station. The overhead cables fizzed and clicked in the wet air.

The station hall was empty and the ticket office was closed. Georgette and Adda-Leigh had been the only passengers to alight at Bernardscar. Now they stood in the station entrance and gazed forlornly out at the rain lashing the gravel forecourt. A narrow road led away from the station. A row of dour-looking shops could just be made out through the downpour. The unlit windows and shuttered doors suggested they weren't open for business.

'Well, we're here now,' said Adda-Leigh. 'We may as well have a look around while we wait for Sam.'

A blustery wind picked up. Adda-Leigh's umbrella was ripped inside out and reduced to a flapping ruin before they'd even crossed the station forecourt.

Georgette wiped the rain from her face and peered up the road ahead of them. Bernardscar was not looking its best. Dark, cramped houses. A rusted metal signpost at a crossroads that pointed the way to the beach. There was a run-down petrol station at the far end of the main street. Beyond it, the road curved away, diving downhill. This must be the road that ran across the thin strip of land connecting Streaming Point to the mainland.

Soaked and thoroughly chilled, the two girls dashed into the first shop they came to that wasn't closed and shuttered against the weather. A bell jangled above the door as they hurried inside.

'You picked a right good 'un for a day trip, didn't you, girls?' A middle-aged woman in a plastic housecoat smiled at them blandly.

Georgette wiped the rainwater from her eyes.

'You're not joking!' said Adda-Leigh. She held up the tattered remains of her umbrella. The woman laughed sympathetically.

The shop sold tinned food, packets of flour, newspapers, cigarettes and sweets. A few sticks of pale pink rock leaned together in a plastic container on the counter. There was a rickety display stand, housing a sparse collection of warped postcards. While Adda-Leigh chatted to the shopkeeper Georgette examined the cards.

There were two that showed Streaming Point. One was a garishly coloured picture from sometime way back in the sixties, showing the mainland beach dotted with holidaymakers, a cobalt blue expanse of sea. The chimneys and concrete buildings of the, at that time, brand-new nuclear power station were clearly visible on the headland across the bay.

The other postcard was a faded reproduction of an old engraving showing Streaming Point a century before the power station had been built. It was all sand dunes and stunted trees. The desolate skyline was interrupted only by an ivy-draped tower with a point-ed roof. It looked like something out of a particularly grim fairy tale. Georgette flipped the card over and read the caption.

Sir Simon de Loup's Folly on Streaming Point, 1855.

She took one of each card over to the counter. Adda-Leigh was buying a packet of extra strong mints.

'It'll take more than mints to warm you up today, duck,' the shopkeeper said.

Georgette held up the postcards and extracted a pound coin from her back pocket.

'Ah, the old folly on Streaming Point.' The shopkeeper shook her head. 'It's still out there you know, what's left of it. They built the power station around it. The folly's in ruins but they still weren't allowed to knock it down. Listed building, you see. And now the power station's shut down too. Of course, they've still got a few security blokes over there. There's some nasty nuclear waste stored there, apparently.'

Georgette nudged Adda-Leigh. 'Did you ask about boat trips?'

'Boat trips? Today?' The shopkeeper raised her eyebrows.

'We saw a poster up at the station. It said there's a boat trip out to look at the grey seals around Streaming Point.'

'Oh no, love. They only run that in the summer. Besides, no one would put out to sea today, not if they've got any sense, what with this storm and all . . . It's lucky we've got that new sea wall. If it weren't for that we'd all be under six feet of water by now, and no mistake.'

Adda-Leigh looked at Georgette. 'We have definitely picked the wrong day to come here.'

The shopkeeper laughed. 'You can say that again! Funny. But you're not the only ones. Today of all days! There was a gang of fellers here earlier. All packed into two of them cross-country jeeps. Tough-looking types. Army, or summut. On manoeuvres, I daresay. One of them popped in for a Snickers bar and a packet of crisps.'

The two girls looked at each other.

'Are you thinking what I'm . . . ?' Georgette began. Adda-Leigh opened her mouth to reply but she didn't get the chance. The sound of a large explosion rattled through the shop.

THE LOST VALLEY

Glamwych. Sam remembered where he'd heard the name. It was a place his father had often spoken about. The drowned village. How a Welsh valley had been flooded to make a reservoir, so the water company could pipe drinking water to English cities. How the local people had no say in the matter. Sam had no interest in the politics, but he couldn't deny the sense of melancholy he felt when he saw the place with his own eyes.

The valley lay some forty miles south-east of his grandmother's house. Sam had left without seeing his father again, and had flown through the cover of thick white cloud. Steep slopes, thick with stunted trees, led down to a vast lake, its surface slate-grey in the cold and sunless afternoon. Sam dropped out of the sky and into the reservoir. He tucked back his wings and entered the water with barely a splash.

He swam down, his dragon eyesight piercing the murky gloom. At the bottom of the reservoir the village still stood. They hadn't bothered to fully demolish all of the houses and cottages or even the church. The roofs had been removed, and anything worth salvaging had been taken away and sold. But the stone walls had been left standing. They provided shelter for shoals of fish and the gardens were now overgrown with waterweed. Sam swam along the course of the old road, and gazed around him. He thought about the people who had lived out their lives in Glamwych, back when it was still a part of the world of humans.

There was no sign that anyone had been back here since the valley had been filled with water. And yet Glamwych had been fresh in Crisp's memory. Somewhere down here there was a sealed room, with water dripping from the ceiling. An underwater headquarters. The lair of Sister Ironspeare. And Sam was going to find it.

He didn't break surface again for over three hours. He had no need to breathe air so he stayed underwater, searching the drowned village and the watery fields that surrounded it for any clue that gave away the presence of the Order.

It wasn't until he was on the verge of giving up that Sam found what he'd been looking for. A little way outside the village was the site of what had once been a large house. Only the four walls remained, and a broken chimney stack, pointing up towards the surface, fifty metres above. Empty windows gaped. Sam swam in through the dark and uninviting doorway. The ground dipped. The floorboards had all rotted away long ago. Silt clogged the stone flags of the old cellar floor. But something caught Sam's eye. A stream of bubbles.

He clawed away a mound of slick, dark mud and found a valve. A shiny metal valve. It was sunk into the stone floor. Sam dug with his clawed hands and feet and with his powerful jaws he ripped up the flagstone and found a shaft sunk into the ground below. He swam down the water-filled shaft and found an airtight door with a circular metal handle. Behind the door was an airlock. The airlock led to a chamber, deep beneath the ground at the bottom of the reservoir. Sam ripped the door off its hinges and let the rush of the water carry him inside.

There was nobody in there. Sam had been sure of it. His senses would have told him if there'd been so much as a mouse hiding behind the airlock door. But there had been someone there recently. Very recently. The Order. Their mark was everywhere. A design, depicting a writhing dragon pierced by a lance, was carved into the back of an ornate wooden chair. Sam demolished it with a snap of his jaws. A bank of computers spat sparks as the water closed over them. The glowing screensavers, showing the Order's badge of the cross, the flame and the pinioned serpent, flickered into darkness. A rack of telephones and mobiles was swept off the wall by the inrushing flood.

Sam was aware that what he was doing was stupid. He should have found some way of getting in without destroying the headquarters. Any clues to the Order's current plans were being obliterated in front of his eyes. But soon he realised what his instinct had known all along. That he would find all the clues he needed just by being in that place.

This one small sealed room had been at the hub of Order activities. It was where Sister Ironspeare had sat, dreaming of finding a precious book on Streaming Point, of inheriting all the power she believed was owed to the Order. Dreaming of being the one leader of the Order of the Pursuing Flame who finally got to preside over the slaying of the last dragon. Echoes of her thoughts and wishes still hung in the space between the walls, even as it filled up with filthy water.

Sam floundered in the waterlogged room. He remembered how when fire had broken out in the kitchen back home and his father's life had been in danger, he'd been afflicted with a vision so powerful he'd been unable to see anything else. Now something like that was happening again.

As he thrashed his limbs in the heaving water, Sam saw a succession of images. Sister Ironspeare monitoring his whereabouts by tracking his use of mobile phone lines. Crisp receiving information on how to find him. Sister Ironspeare again deep in discussion with the major. A plan being formulated to launch an attack on Streaming Point, where an artefact she called the Book of the Last was hidden. And a bogus text message being sent to Adda-Leigh's mobile phone — *Meet me in Bernardscar*. Finally, Sam saw a series of explosions that released a boiling sea. Struggling in the flooded room, Sam could see nothing but the visions his mind was showing him. Visions of sheets of fire and torrents of water. But beyond these flickering images he remembered his dreams of Adda-Leigh, drowning. His limbs heavy with dread, he groped his way towards the broken doorway of the room beneath the reservoir floor.

HIGH TIDE

They heard a series of loud explosions and then a terrible, seething roar. It was the tide breaking over the village. The sea came surging down the quiet roads, boiled across the fields and burst into buildings. All but the heaviest, most secure objects in its path were simply swept away.

There was no time to think, no time to stand amazed or wonder what had happened. All Georgette and Adda-Leigh could do was to follow the shopkeeper as she led them through a door behind the counter and up a flight of stairs. From there they climbed up a ladder into the loft and then through a skylight on to the roof. The girls both had mobiles but they could get no signal. They were stranded.

Adda-Leigh looked at Georgette's face. Her skin

was pink with the cold.

'Well, we've got a nice view from up here, at least.'

Beyond the churning waves around the broken sea wall lay Streaming Point, now cut off by an expanse of heaving sea. The chimneys and rectangular buildings of the old power station were clearly visible against the rugged contours of the land.

'Sorry, but I don't want to admire the scenery.' Georgette frowned and looked hard at her friend. 'You did hear them, didn't you? The explosions, I mean.'

'Maybe it was just the noise of the sea, smashing through the wall?'

'They were explosions, Addy. Bombs. Deliberately planted and detonated where they'd cause maximum damage.' Georgette chewed her lower lip and shivered. 'Somebody blew up the sea wall.'

Adda-Leigh gripped the roof tiles with her chilled fingers and looked down.

'But why would anyone do that? Do you think it was the Order?'

'I don't know,' Georgette said. 'I just want to get out of here.'

A helicopter hovered above the devastated village like a monstrous dragonfly. Then it moved out to sea, heading towards Streaming Point.

The dark water swilled around the walls of the terrace, slopping against the ground-floor windows.

Where the road had been, the water ran fast and deep, carrying great rafts of flotsam. Broken fences, splintered timber, oil drums, plastic bottles and bags, all went boiling along in the torrent.

'Oh, you poor ducks!' The shopkeeper, still in her plastic housecoat, was sitting astride the roof as if it was something she did every day. 'Your parents will be worried sick!' The woman smiled blandly.

Adda-Leigh pushed the braids out of her eyes. 'Well at least it's stopped raining!' she said to Georgette.

Georgette gave a hollow laugh.

There was a shout from somewhere close by and they turned to look. A rubber raft was navigating its way across the flooded back gardens. It sailed around the tops of fruit trees and past some sagging fence posts protruding from the water.

'Rescue!'

'About time too!' The shopkeeper stood up and waved. 'Over here, you daft ha'p'orths! We're here! Come on, girls, we'd best get ourselves to the back of the roof.'

Georgette and Adda-Leigh began to follow the shopkeeper across the tiles when a sudden gust of wind hit the building. Adda-Leigh was caught off balance. With a sense of horrified disbelief she felt herself toppling backwards.

For a brief instant, she saw her own panic reflected

in Georgette's wide-eyed stare and outstretched arms. She pitched and fell, hitting the tiles hard. Winded and disorientated, she rolled over and over, bowling down the slippery roof. The metal gutter dug into her back and she let out a gasp of pain. Then there was nothing beneath her and she was falling through the empty air.

SPINOZA'S WORM

Qua knew everything. He knew about Sam. He knew that Aaron had seen his old schoolfriend after the changes overtook him, that he'd witnessed what Sam had become. He knew the histories of Luhngdou Island and of the Order of the Pursuing Flame.

Aaron listened, open-mouthed.

Qua smiled. 'Do you know the writings of Spinoza?'

Aaron shook his head.

'I have a great passion for Western philosophy. There's something so pleasingly exotic about it, don't you think?' The old man's eyes sparkled.

Aaron cleared his throat. 'You what?' he said.

'Spinoza once wrote of a little worm, trapped inside the bloodstream of some much larger creature. The worm travels through veins and arteries, sees the white cells and the red cells and the various wonders of the circulatory system. But it has no idea that they are all part of one single being. You, Aaron, are something like that worm.'

'Hold up! You're saying I'm a worm?'

'Spinoza's worm, yes. Your head is in a whirl from the things I have told you because you are unable to see the true nature of things. The vastness of everything is beyond you. This is not your fault. I have several advantages over you. I have studied these matters all my life, for one thing. For another, I am pure Luhngdonese, and although I am not of the dragon-folk, I do possess some of their attributes. Spending many years in the company of one of them has seen to that.'

'Eh?' Aaron said.

'I am a reader of minds. And I have some foreknowledge of things to come.'

Aaron took a deep breath.

'Even Sam can't do that,' he said, a little shakily.

'Perhaps not, when last you met him. But the dragon-folk develop over time and in many stages. He is still young. He may live a thousand years and still not master all his potential skills.'

'You're doing my head in!' Aaron moaned and slapped a hand to his forehead. Then he looked up, brows puckered, as another thought occurred to him.

'So how come my mum suddenly decided to take in a lodger the minute you turned up?'

Qua looked away and gave a little cough. 'I also have the power to . . . encourage positive thoughts in others. I only use it in exceptional circumstances.'

'Sam can't do that either.'

Qua shuffled his sandalled feet. 'It probably hasn't occurred to him to try. It is not, I confess, the most ethical of practices.'

Aaron stood up. 'Too true. That was well out of order! Why couldn't you just stay in a hotel or something like a normal tourist?'

'I am not here for a holiday, Aaron. I have to find Fen.'

'Who?'

'I know where she will be. There is a meeting point. A place where lives intersect. It is a place that exerts a strong pull. That is where I must go. As for coming to London first, well, I needed to know more about your former schoolfriend Sam Lim-Evans and hoped I would be able to find the necessary information if I came to his home town. I have gleaned much from your mind, Aaron.'

Aaron put his hands on his hips. 'Now hang on a bit! I don't think I like the idea of you rummaging through my brain like it's the bargain bin at the local jumble sale!'

'Much of what I needed was information you didn't even know you had.'

'That's not the point.'

Qua sighed. 'Very well. Please accept my apologies. And now, if you will excuse me, we must pack.'

'You're leaving?' Aaron was surprised. 'Well, so you should. After what you told me about messing with my mum's mind.'

'We shall be travelling north. We must arrive at the meeting point in good time.'

'Hold on a minute. Did you say "we"?'

'Of course. I am a stranger in a strange land. I may have certain extra-sensory powers, but in other ways I am as helpless as a child. I shall need you to accompany me. We shall travel north.'

'North? You can't just go north! Where exactly do you want to go?'

'I shall know the place when we arrive there.'

'No way! You're mad! There's absolutely no way anyone's going anywhere with you!'

'If we do not go soon, then your friends Georgette and Adda-Leigh, and the dragon-boy Sam himself, they all may die.' Qua folded his hands in his lap and looked up at Aaron. His gaze was steady. But for once his face bore no trace of a smile.

BLACK RAIN FALLING

Fen swam past the headland. By day she kept out of sight, submerged in the chill coastal waters, swimming through the shallows, around and around. By night she flew, gliding on outstretched wings, watching the rocky shore, the silent sand dunes, the buildings with their tanks and towers and electric lights.

The power station excited her. She could sense the unstable nature of the materials stored there. The humans had nowhere else to keep them. They had abandoned the power station, closed it down and shut it up. But the deadly waste they'd created still remained. Humans were such fools. They planted the seeds of their own downfall wherever they went.

The potential for destruction that lay within the concrete walls, inside the sealed tanks, was vast. Fen was reminded of a place she'd found on her travels, somewhere along the endless sprawling borders between Europe and Asia. There'd been an accident, many years before, at a power plant like the one on Streaming Point. Radiation had been released and a poisonous cloud had drifted into the air. Humans had abandoned the plant, and all the land for miles around it. Fen had exalted in their absence, delighting in the ghostly echo of human fear that she could sense still hanging in the air. She basked in the faint crackle of radiation she could detect all around her.

She wanted space. Yearned for it, with an instinctive desire that went beyond her own understanding. The only way she could think of getting it was to rid this crowded planet of some of its most unappetising inhabitants, the humans.

And here, around Streaming Point, she could taste the same dry crackle. It was like an itchy kind of static, permeating both air and water. Fen still didn't know why she'd been drawn to the headland. But she hoped that before she left she might find an opportunity to release some of the power that lay dormant there, to channel it into heat, to send it boiling into the sea, streaming into clouds that would turn to black rain, and fall like poison on the land.

CROSSING PEAKS

The cloud lifted and Sam saw the rugged countryside spread out below him. A series of great hills, all cut with rushing streams, stretched away for miles. There was barely a solitary farmhouse to be seen in all directions. The nearest sign of human habitation was a length of dry-stone wall enclosing a circle of weathered menhirs, laid out by a long-forgotten people for a purpose now equally unknown.

He'd tried to contact Georgette and Adda-Leigh, assembling the familiar patterns and codes, seeking out the correct frequency, the relay of cells that would allow him to transmit his spoken thoughts directly into a particular mobile phone. But neither girl could be contacted. Wherever they were, there was no signal available. He had to get to them himself. And the only place he could think of to look was Streaming Point. His jangling senses told him he wouldn't be wrong.

Sam dropped low, and followed the contour of the land, flying with his belly just a few metres above the withered grass. He crossed black bogs and outcrops of wet rock. A few bedraggled sheep watched him pass, but otherwise his presence went unseen. The peaks rose into another bank of low-lying cloud and Sam followed the slope up into the cold and clammy blankness.

There was a new strength in him. His wings beat the damp air and forced the elements to give way. He tore through the sky, crossing mountain, moor and lake, and he brushed aside the smothering clouds. Fire blazed in his chest and at the back of his throat, but a chill calm had descended on him.

'Fly, Sammy!' That's what Grandma Evans had said. 'Fly, now. Make sure everything's all right with your Adda-Leigh. Otherwise you'll not get a moment's peace of mind, wherever you go.'

He'd been right to go to Grandma Evans. He'd needed someone to tell him what to do. Despite his terrifying appearance, despite his awesome powers, he was still just a boy at heart.

As for his father, Sam could only push Llew to the back of his mind. The gunshot wound had healed, and Sam could sense that his body had somehow grown even stronger because of it. His scales had thickened, grown denser in number and were now tougher than ever. He didn't think a bullet would be able to penetrate his hide again.

But still Sam was in pain. How could he bear to even think about his father after all that had happened in Wales? He buried the question and turned his thoughts to the north-east. Letting instinct and all six senses guide him, Sam hurtled on towards the Yorkshire coast, and Adda-Leigh.

GNOME FLOTILLA

Georgette screamed, standing on the tiles with her arms stretched uselessly in front of her as if to reach out and grab Adda-Leigh and pull her back to safety. But she was too late, her friend had already fallen. She could only watch her tumble off the roof.

Georgette waited for the splash but none came. Instead there were voices. Then a second rubber raft appeared. It had arrived below them without their noticing and had been out of sight, close to the walls of the house. Adda-Leigh lay in the bottom of the raft. A rescue worker was bent over her. His fluorescent life jacket had the words YORKSHIRE COAST VOLUNTEER FIRE SERVICE printed across it.

Georgette scrambled down the tiles towards them. Two drainpipes were fixed to the side of the house;

one was iron, the other, larger pipe was of grey plastic. Georgette heard one of the rescue workers call out a warning, but she ignored it. Before she had time to think she'd swung her legs over the guttering and was climbing down towards the raft. Her foot found one of the pipe brackets fixed into the brickwork. She lowered herself down.

'Come on then, lass. Easy now. We've got you.'

She felt strong arms guide her into the raft. The flimsy craft pitched and rolled as she clambered into it.

'By heck, you girls are eager to get off that roof, aren't you? First this one decides to throw herself into the raft from a great height, and now you come shinning down the drainpipe! I hope your mother's a bit more civilised!'

'Our mother?' said Adda-Leigh. She looked up at where the shopkeeper still stood, the wind plucking at her housecoat. She giggled.

Georgette looked at her. 'If she's our mum then that makes us sisters.'

She had to fight back the urge to join in Adda-Leigh's laughter. But she recognised the edge of hysteria in her friend's giggling fit. Their escape from the sudden flood and Adda-Leigh's tumble from the roof had left them both in a state of shock. She took a deep breath.

'What do you think's going on? If the Order have

flooded the village they must have a reason. The headland must be cut off. Maybe they're going to –'

Georgette broke off. Adda-Leigh had stopped laughing and was shivering instead.

'You're not hurt or anything?' Georgette frowned.

But Adda-Leigh forced a smile. 'I'm fine. Pretty lucky, huh?'

'Lucky's not the word, I tell thee,' the rescue worker broke in, shaking his head. 'You don't want to fall into that water. There's all sorts in there. Raw sewage. Untreated chemicals . . .'

' . . . Garden gnomes,' said Adda-Leigh. She pointed. Close by the raft, half a dozen plastic gnomes were bobbing on the water, their wide eyes and red painted lips smiling up at the grey sky.

Now both girls dissolved into helpless, shrieking laughter. All the pent-up tension of their situation found its release in wild, uncontrollable mirth at the sight of a flotilla of gnomes.

The rescue worker shook his head again. 'Daft, the both of you!' he said.

They were still laughing when a third boat pulled up alongside them. The rescue rafts had moved out of the flooded gardens into the field beyond, a field that now resembled a wide lake. Georgette and Adda-Leigh were in one boat. The shopkeeper, wrapped in a blanket, sat in the other.

The third boat was larger, with a fibreglass hull. And it was fitted with an outboard motor. Adda-Leigh heard Georgette draw in her breath. A man was crouched in the stern, one hand on the tiller. His other arm was outstretched, pointing at the rescue workers in the raft. In his trembling hand he held a pistol fitted with a silencer.

GREEN BOTTLES

Aaron sat hunched in the back of the car, squashed between the constantly fidgeting Dawn on one side and the bony frame of Qua on the other. They were stuck in yet another traffic jam.

Aaron's father gripped the steering wheel and shook his head. 'This'll take a while,' he said for the umpteenth time.

'Never mind. How about a sing-song?'

'No! Please!' Aaron wrung his hands.

Dawn dug him in the ribs. 'Don't be such a grump, Aaron.'

'But can't you see what's happened! It's Qua. He's brainwashed the lot of you!'

Aaron's mother looked puzzled. 'Mister Qua's our lodger. He's always prompt with his rent, aren't you, Mister Qua?'

Qua nodded slowly.

'Exactly! He's the lodger! Who ever heard of taking the lodger on a last-minute family holiday? And since when did we ever go on last-minute holidays, anyway?'

'Come on, Aaron. Where's your sense of adventure?'

'A camping holiday in a disaster zone? In February? That sounds like a bit too much adventure for me. I'm only going because of . . .' Aaron was going to mention Sam but he broke off. He couldn't face the thought of trying to explain Sam's transformation to the rest of his family, especially in their current collective state of mind. Nobody seemed to take in a word he said.

'Who wants a toffee?' Aaron's mother delved into her large handbag.

Dawn squealed and bounced up and down on the seat.

'Leave off, Dawn!' Aaron sighed and stuck a hand into the bag of sweets his mother held out. But Dawn got there first. Their mother snatched the bag away.

'Now, now! One at a time, please!'

'Oh never mind.' Aaron held his head in his hands. 'I'm not even hungry.'

In the driving seat Aaron's father started to sing.

'Ten green bottles hanging on the wall! Ten green bottles hanging on the wall! And if one green bottle . . . !'

As the rest of his family joined in, loudly, tunelessly, Aaron, his features etched with pain, glanced up and saw the wrinkled face of Qua regarding him.

'This isn't going to work, you know.' Aaron tried to ignore his family's caterwauling. 'There's no way we're going to be able to drive all the way into that flooded village.'

Aaron's parents had shaken him awake that morning, saying they were taking a trip to the north to see the Yorkshire disaster zone for themselves. The idea was preposterous.

'There'll be roadblocks and all sorts. Or they might think we're looters and shoot us!'

The news was just breaking on the car radio. The sea wall had collapsed in a place called Bernardscar, near the Streaming Point nuclear power station, and the village was being evacuated. No one in the family seemed interested in discussing how they'd all known about the flooding of Bernardscar some three hours before it actually happened.

Aaron glared at Qua. 'You're heading for a world of trouble, I'm telling you!' he said.

The old man smiled serenely. 'We shall see,' he said.

Aaron shook his head and clamped his hands over his ears. There were still another eight bottles to go.

BORN TO KILL

Fen lay just below the surface of the water and watched the coastguard rescue vessel moving across the bay, heading for the flooded streets of Bernardscar. She could sense the thoughts of the humans on board, their hopes of evacuating the village and saving lives. It disgusted her.

Humans were simple to kill, with their soft skin so easily torn open, with their thin bones and watery blood. Weak. For Fen, the word defined humanity. And yet she'd been human herself once.

Her memories began with a little girl, her laughter echoing around the rock formations as she knelt above the body of a bat, clutching a sharpened flint in her hand. She'd killed things, even then.

She remembered roaming the caves on her little stick

legs, which carried her tiny fragile body with its small and clouded mind. Thinking back now, she could hardly believe she'd survived in such a puny state. But it was only when the changes came upon her that she really understood how weak she'd been in human form.

She'd exalted in the transformation. Scale, claw, tooth and wing. She'd read the old man's mind and knew that she'd been imprisoned, locked away, buried alive. Only then had she understood that the caves were not large enough to contain her. They were just an egg, a womb in which she'd been gestating for the past fouteen years. It was time to be born.

Was there a place in her heart for the child she'd once been? Some sense of regret over the twisted years she'd spent below ground? Fen would never have admitted to it. But when she thought of her early years a feeling of panic and distress would run through her. It made her want to lash out, to kill something weaker than she was. To kill humans.

Until a year ago, the only human she'd known was Qua. But out here in the world they were everywhere. She wanted to clear them away. On Streaming Point, inside the sealed containers, the nuclear waste called out to her, singing its wild static song of clicks and buzzes. Perhaps there was a way to clear a great space, to create the emptiness she craved. Perhaps that was why she was here.

She swept towards the coastguard vessel, accelerating as she approached. She sensed the alarm as the crew caught sight of the disturbance in the water and it pleased her. They were right to be afraid. There would be no rescue here.

Reaching the boat, she sank her claws into the hull and dragged it back out into deeper water. She stilled the gibbering clamour of the crew with one sharp word, uttered telepathically, filling the minds of the men on board.

'Silence!'

She rarely meddled with human thought. The minds of men disgusted her. And yet it served her purpose on occasions such as this. And so it was that a message was sent out from the coastguard vessel ordering the suspension of the rescue mission. All coastguard units were stood down. Conditions were said to be too dangerous for any further efforts to be made at this time.

Fen left the crew sitting on the deck of their boat, heads lolling, their minds empty. And she tore a ragged hole in the hull of the vessel before she swam away.

EMPTY GROUND

Far to the south, the marsh grasses bend in the wind, just as they have for thousands of years.

This is the site, the place where they found the body. The archaeologists have all gone. They dug here for as long as they were allowed, searching for anything else they could find connected with the long-dead boy and his vanished people. But they found nothing.

Soon the men from the water board will return to complete the work they were doing when they first found the body. But for now, the site remains deserted, just another patch of marshy ground.

Wind ripples the grass. Rain falls. There is a hazy shifting in the air, barely distinguishable from the weather. And she appears.

A woman. Short and slight, with long black hair

that blows in the marsh breeze. She glances, once, at the empty ground. And then she turns her head slowly and looks across the marsh, towards the office blocks of Docklands. Although it is too far away to be seen by ordinary eyes, her piercing gaze is turned in the direction of the laboratory buildings of the department of human archaeology, North-East London University.

ONE PIECE OF ROPE

Adda-Leigh looked at Georgette. 'I can't believe it. It's happening again. Anyone would think I went around with a big label stuck to my forehead saying "Please Kidnap Me"!'

'This'll be the last time. Count on it.' Crisp had to shout to make himself heard over the splutter of the outboard motor. He kept the pistol trained on the two girls as best he could, but the boat reared each time it hit a wave, and his gun hand jerked alarmingly with every jolt.

Crisp had ordered the rescue workers and the woman from the shop to climb on to the nearest rooftop. The gun in his hand made him difficult to argue with. He'd taken a knife from his pocket and slashed holes in both the inflatable rafts. Air had hissed and bubbled out of them and they'd sunk beneath the dirty water. Then he'd successfully steered his boat out across Bernardscar promenade and through the wreckage of the sea wall. This had been achieved more by luck than judgement. It was clear he was no sailor. Adda-Leigh guessed he'd stolen the boat, or found it abandoned at the edge of the floods.

'Where are you taking us? What are you going to do?' Georgette couldn't keep the panic out of her voice.

'Shut your mouth!' Crisp waved his pistol and pointed to a length of nylon rope lying coiled in the bottom of the boat. 'Tie her up!' He pointed the gun at Adda-Leigh, then at Georgette to ensure she carried out his order. With shaking hands, Georgette picked up the rope.

'Tie it good and tight!'

'Sorry, Addy.' Georgette pulled the rope taut and drew the ends into a knot.

Adda-Leigh looked at Crisp. One of his eyes was twitching uncontrollably. He probably hadn't eaten or slept in days. There was a livid red burn on the back of one hand.

'There's only one piece of rope,' said Adda-Leigh. Georgette had gone very pale. 'Are you okay, girl?'

Crisp cut the boat's engine. They were over halfway to Streaming Point, now made an island by the flood, but they were still in deep water. The boat rose and fell on the rolling waves.

'I feel sick,' Georgette said. She lowered her head and leaned out over the side of the boat.

Crisp shook his head. 'My mission is to kill the filthy alien dragon. The Order told me to do it, and I'm going to show them I know my duty. Doesn't matter what they tried to do to me. I don't go easy.' He took a firmer grip on his pistol and squinted at Adda-Leigh. 'And you're going to help me do it. I recognise you. Where you are, the dragon always appears. And when he does, I'll be waiting for him. This time, the dragon dies. So you're important.' He turned to Georgette. 'But you're not. So we only need one piece of rope.'

'Georgette! Look out!' Adda-Leigh's scream of warning came too late. Crisp leaned forward and with a sweep of his arm, pushed Georgette over the side and into the water. Then he restarted the motor and the boat moved on, heading towards the breakers crashing on to the shores of Streaming Point.

END OF THE ROAD

The police van was parked in the middle of the road. Plastic cones, fluorescent orange smeared with dried mud, were lined across the turning from the hedgerow on one side to the poplar trees on the other. A policeman, wearing a high-visibility jacket with COMMUNITY OFFICER written across the chest, was leaning against the bonnet of his van.

'Ah,' said Aaron's father. 'Hmm. Looks like the end of the road, folks.'

He brought the car to a halt. The policeman looked over at them.

Qua leaned forward. 'Perhaps you could take a less obvious route.'

'Watch it, Dad!' Aaron cast a nervous glance at Qua. 'Don't let him talk you into doing something weird.'

But Aaron's father shrugged. 'Could be worth a try, Qua. I mean, we've got ourselves to Yorkshire. Seems a shame to come all this way and not get so much as a peep at these famous floods.'

He started the car and drove past the policeman, who took a few paces forward and stood with his arms folded, watching them with a blank expression until they rounded the bend and were out of sight.

When they'd gone about five hundred metres further along the road, Qua sat forward again. He pointed at an open gate leading into a field. 'There!'

'Right you are!'

The car turned sharply with a shriek of brakes. Aaron was thrown on to Dawn, who let out a muffled squeal. She pummelled his back with both fists.

'Leave it out, Dawn! Slow down, Dad! Tell him, Mum! Qua, you nut-job, stop messing about!' Aaron was yelling as loud as he could. But so was everyone else in the car. Everyone except Qua.

They bounced across the rutted field.

'Hold on, everyone!'

'Dad! The hedge!'

There was a sickening thump as they went careering into a thicket of hawthorns. Twigs and branches lashed at the windscreen and scraped against the bodywork. The car wheels spun and the engine coughed and retched. And suddenly they were through the hedge and out the other side.

'Blimey,' somebody said, quietly. Spread out before them was a stretch of dark water. Here and there, trees and hedges and the stranded posts of washed-away fences jutted out like the broken fingers of drowning giants, pointing at the sky. They had reached the edge of the flood.

The car bumped down a sodden, grassy slope.

'Brake, Dad! Brake!'

The engine sputtered and died.

'Ah,' said Aaron's father. His hands gripped the steering wheel. He pumped the brake pedal. But the car slipped on the waterlogged slope and slid down towards the filthy water. Silence fell inside the vehicle. 'Hmm,' said Aaron's father.

STRAWS

Fen had read the old man's mind before she left the caverns. She'd seen his memories. She knew the truth. Slithering through the rancid flood, she recalled what she knew, running the stolen memory through her mind like a home movie.

The group had met in the darkness of a moonless night, out on the mountainside, hunkered down in the shelter of an outcrop of rocks. Seven Luhngdonese elders. The last of their kind, returning one final time to the land of their ancestors, a little island in the South China Sea known as Luhngdou.

'But can we be sure there is no other?'

'We can never be absolutely sure. Perhaps the strain is stronger than we know? Perhaps the dragon-seed will lie dormant in even our most distant descendants, only to emerge again in time?'

'That cannot be. We are the last of the true Luhng-donese. Those that leave the island, who intermarry with foreigners, who spoil the purity of our blood, they would never be blessed with the dragon-strain. Never!'

'The Order will hunt them down, nonetheless.'

'The Order is intent on genocide. But they are fools as well as murderers. No cross-breed could ever sire one of the dragon-folk!'

'And what of the Companions?'

'They can no longer be trusted. Their ranks have been infiltrated by our enemies.'

'I heard they have a priest among their number, a man of Luhngdonese descent. A certain Father David?'

'He is no pure-blood! His father was Chinese. Besides, as a priest he has taken a vow of chastity. He will have no heirs. No. Be assured. We are the last. And when the child is born there will be no more.'

The woman clutched her swollen midriff. The six other elders were all men.

'You may die in childbirth,' one of them said to her. 'You and the child. You are not a young woman. Birth can be risky at your age. And with your condition . . .'

'Bluntly put.' The woman sniffed. 'You may as well all know. I have the weakness of the heart that afflicts the female line of our people. My death is likely. But I do not believe the child will die. We have all devoted our lives to studying this matter. There isn't a family tree we haven't traced, not a single incident of the dragon-change that hasn't been noted. The child I am carrying is the last pure-blood Luhngdonese in the world. According to all the signs and predictions, backed up by all our studies and calculations, this child will be of the dragon-kind. The Order will kill us without hesitation, and worse, they may use my child in their own dark rituals. This I cannot allow. You must find the ancient hiding places of our people. One of you must agree to go into hiding with the infant, to rear the child as best you can, to manage matters when the dragon-change occurs. You have the straws, Qua? Good. Give them to me. You shall all draw lots.'

Fen swam beneath the bloated carcass of a drowned cow floating calmly on the surface of the water. She felt a powerful sense of nervous anticipation. Something was on its way, but what it was she couldn't tell.

She reached the ruins of the sea wall and with a powerful sweep of her tail propelled herself up and out of the water, scrambling over the shattered concrete, dragging her scaled belly across twisted railings and broken paving slabs. She crossed the broken wall and plunged into the sea.

Of the seven elders of the island, only Qua now

remained alive. Fen had sought them all in vain. Her mother had, indeed, died shortly after she was born. One by one, the other five had fallen victim to the agents of the Order of the Pursuing Flame. Qua and Fen had remained hidden, safe beneath the mountain rock of Luhngdou. But what had it all been for? Was it true, that she was the last of her kind? Why had she been spared, only to live out her days on this festering planet, polluted, as it was, by humanity?

Her early years had been spent shut away in an underground prison. Now she'd tasted freedom her appetite was insatiable. She needed to be free of people. She needed space. Her instinct had brought her here. Was Streaming Point the place she'd be able to make her own? Somewhere she could breathe. A place wiped clean of humanity.

With the blood tingling in her veins, she headed back out towards the headland.

THE THING IN THE WATER

He'd flown across the moors and then on, to the flood-wracked Yorkshire coast. Now Sam lay half-submerged in the oily water of a drowned shore-side meadow. He lifted his head, bent his back, flexed his wings and shook the moisture from their leathery skin. He looked towards the village. The water lapped at the top-floor windows of the houses and shops. He could make out a few people stranded on the roofs. No efforts were being made to rescue them as far as he could see. In fact, some of the stranded people looked like rescue workers themselves.

He looked out to sea, towards Streaming Point. He saw the battered concrete chimneys and low, rectangular buildings of the old power station. A helicopter was landing there, lowering itself down like a giant wasp settling on a picnic table. Beyond lay the open occan.

And there was something else out there, between the shoreline and Streaming Point, something moving just below the surface. A disturbance in the water was raising a trail of bubbles. Whatever it was, it was very big and it was moving fast.

Sam turned his face away. A shiver ran through him. The thing in the water disturbed him. There was something familiar and yet strange about it, like when he was a boy and he'd caught sight of the back of his own head in a bathroom fitted with several mirrors. It felt wrong, as if it was something he shouldn't be seeing, himself as a stranger. The thing in the sea gave off the same vibration, except a hundred times stronger. He was glad it was swimming out to sea. If he was lucky, it would never come back.

Sam closed his eyes and let his mind reach out, searching for Adda-Leigh. This was where she'd been told to meet him. And the place had turned into a disaster area. The helicopter hovering over the headland was the only sign of any rescue effort he could see. He knew that Adda-Leigh was alive, at least. He could sense she was here. But where, exactly?

Sam expected the instinctive knowledge of her whereabouts to form in his mind. Instead he encountered something very different. Startled, he slipped, lost his footing and gave a grunt. A puff of smoke was forced from one nostril and he choked, his body convulsing, his tail thrashing, churning the shallow water.

Visions flickered through his mind. Sam groaned and shook his head wildly. Adda-Leigh, underwater. Sister Ironspeare, her lips curled in a cruel smile. Crisp, wild-eyed, a gun at his head. The major, laughing as he pulled the trigger. And Adda-Leigh again, her body still, lifeless, suspended in deep water. It struck him then, in a moment of painful realisation. This stretch of flooded coastline was where Adda-Leigh was going to die. Unless he, Sam, could somehow make sure it didn't happen. He had to find her first.

Desperately, he tried to focus on the real world. He opened his eyes wide and stared up at the cloud-filled sky. He bit down hard on his tongue and tasted blood. But it was no good. His vision filled with turquoise light and he was underwater again, only this time something was different. There was no sign of Adda-Leigh.

Sam had the impression of rapid movement, as if he were racing at great speed through the depths of the sea. Nothing remained in focus. A feeling of dread began to grow in him as he sped onward.

And then he saw it, up ahead. Something moving in the water. A presence. It was heading towards him. He couldn't turn away, though every fibre of his being was screaming for him to do so. A last wild rush and there it was looming in front of him. He felt a jarring pain and thrashed out with his claws.

Sam opened his eyes. He was still in the flooded meadow. He had coiled himself into a circle and he had bitten deep into the tip of his own tail. His blood was darkening the filthy water, spreading red through the rusty brown. The pain was intense and his jaw ached. His newly toughened scales, now thicker than ever, could resist almost anything it seemed, except the power of his own teeth, a dragon's bite.

He lay back and let the water hold him. The visions had cleared, for the time being, but he was left exhausted. The memory of what he'd seen was etched into his mind.

It was something new, something he'd not encountered before, and nothing had prepared him for the shock. It had thrown him back into the helpless state he'd experienced when he'd first undergone the dragon-change. He had searched with his mind for Adda-Leigh but he had found something else instead.

He'd seen a face in the water. A face pressed close to his. A face like his own. A dragon's face. A spine-topped cranium, an elongated muzzle, jaws lined with rows of teeth, skin puckered with crusted scales. He could have been looking in a mirror, except that was something he never did.

He'd always been told he was the last of his kind. Even the Order believed that to be the case. And yet there was another. Another dragon, the same as Sam. Except the startled eyes that had stared into his for the split second before he'd broken out of the trance were not like his own. They were wild eyes, angry and disturbed. But they were not the eyes of either a monster or a fifteen-year-old youth from London. They were the eyes of a girl.

DOWN AND DOWN

Georgette kicked out, fighting the pull of the current. She broke the surface, gasping and spluttering. A wave swamped her immediately. Clawing at the water, she pushed her face clear of the swell for another precious gulp of air.

The sea was deep and achingly cold. The intense chill of it was sapping her of all strength. Even with her head above water she was finding it hard to breathe. She heard the boat's engine receding into the distance. She heard seagulls calling. Waves breaking on the shore. It didn't matter. It all sounded far away. Too far away.

The sea swell lifted her up and dropped her down. The grey water broke over her head once more. She felt herself sinking, down and down into ice-cold darkness.

EDGE OF THE WATER

The car was embedded nose-first in the muddy water. The front seats were submerged and fetid brown ooze lapped at the windows. Only the rear of the vehicle was above the water level, but the back wheels were gradually sinking in the thick mud.

The boot was open. Everything Aaron's family had packed had been removed. And they'd brought plenty. Twenty or so metres back up the slope, where the ground was relatively dry, they'd set up camp.

Dawn was in the tent, reading a comic. Aaron's mother was sitting in a deckchair with a magazine open in front of her. Aaron's father had the camping stove on the go, and was busy frying sausages.

'Shame about the car,' he said. 'But no real harm done. We all got out in one piece. Nothing wrong that a set of dry clothes can't fix. And here we've got a decent view of the floods.' He shook the pan, shifting the sausages in the hot fat. 'Now all we need's a bit of sunshine!'

Aaron's mother lowered her magazine. 'Well, it's stopped raining, at least. Can't expect miracles. After all, it's not really springtime yet.'

'It's nearly March though. In like a lion, out like a lamb. That's what they say about March. Or is that April?'

Aaron listened to them in numbed silence, but all the while his eyes were trained on Qua, out in the flood. The old man had been gone for hours but now here he was, returning with something he'd found, or possibly even made himself. He was on a raft made from a panel of old fencing, stout wooden planks still firmly nailed to two thick posts. A couple of oil drums had been strapped to the planks for extra buoyancy, but it still looked a precarious craft. Qua held a long metal pole in both hands and was punting the raft over the floodwater towards the sunken car. He called out, 'Aaron! I need your help. We have to go on. We are close, but we are not yet at the meeting place.'

Aaron shook his head. 'You're joking, right?'

Qua pushed the raft closer. 'Your friend Sam Lim-Evans will need my help if he is to survive the trial that awaits him. And so you must help me get to him.

I am an old man and cannot manage this raft alone.'

'You don't seem to be doing too badly,' Aaron muttered.

'Besides, would you not want to see him again? One last time?' Qua had almost reached the flood-line. His nut-brown forehead was beaded with sweat. Punting was clearly hard work.

'What d'you mean, "one last time"?'

Qua leant on his pole and smiled. 'You must come with me, Aaron.'

Aaron looked at his parents.

His mother shook her magazine. 'Go on, Aaron. Go with Mr Qua.'

'Yeah. You give the old feller a hand, son.' His father shook the sausages in the pan again.

Aaron puffed out his cheeks. 'Mum. Dad. Don't you think I might be putting myself in danger if I go with Qua?'

'Don't be silly, love. You'll be fine.'

Aaron shrugged. He wished he felt as blithely unconcerned as his parents did. Qua was clearly still influencing their thoughts. Aaron took a deep breath and clenched his fists. I'm doing this for Sam, for Georgette, for Adda-Leigh, he told himself.

Qua manoeuvred the raft into the water margin, and grounded it amongst the clumps of grass that jutted from the shallows. Aaron took a deep breath.

There was a hollow feeling in the pit of his stomach. He only had Qua's word that Sam was involved at all. Could he trust the old man, when Qua had been brainwashing Aaron's whole family from the moment they'd first set eyes on him? There was only one way to find out. Aaron stepped on to the raft, which tilted unsteadily under his feet.

'I'll save you a sausage, Aaron,' he heard his father call out. 'For when you get back.'

SAND SKIN

Fen scrambled blindly across the seaweed-slicked rocks of Streaming Point. Her head reeled. What was it, the thing that had seen her? It had seen her with its mind, seen her in a way only she should be able to see. The old man had a few tricks up his sleeve, it was true. Living with Fen for so long had seen to that. But she would know Qua anywhere. This was something else. Something impure. Like her and yet not like her. A freak. She'd fled from it, sickened by the touch of its mind.

She burrowed into the pebble-strewn beach, instinctively trying to hide herself beneath the ground. Her skin, still wet from the sea, was soon caked in sand. The dry grains stuck to her scales, coating her in a dull layer of grit, like a new skin. She stopped digging.

Wait, she told herself. Of course! This headland was a meeting place. Her instinct told her so. A point where all lines met. There was more to it than nuclear rain and the destruction of some human settlements. Much more. And it had already begun. Men were here, ready to fight and die on this three-mile stretch of sand and rock.

Qua had thought of her as the last of her kind, and so she was. The last pure breed. But now there was this other. This misbegotten thing. This mutation. And she would meet with it here, on the headland. It would have to be destroyed. She knew that, with the certainty of instinct. It was here that the mutant dragon-boy would die.

III

Face of the Deep

THE SURFACE

Laboratory of the Department of Human Archaeology
North-East London University

Evening has come. The department is closed and the laboratory is empty. A telephone rings on a deserted desk. The strident tones echo forlornly along the damp corridor and through the cold, white-walled rooms, where the air hangs heavy with the smell of preserving fluid.

The ringing of the telephone cuts off and the echoes die away to silence.

But who is this? A figure stands by the laboratory door. A woman steps out of the shadows, her long black hair shifting, as if touched by a gentle breeze. But the laboratory is still as the grave.

A specimen lies in a tank of preservative, awaiting further examination. The dead youth, dredged from a marsh. The department is intent on delving into all his secrets. They'll rummage through the contents of his stomach, search his nostrils for traces of ancient airborne pollen, rifle through every organ in his body in their quest for knowledge. Or so they intend.

Without making a sound, the woman steps across the room and places her hand gently against the surface of the preserving tank.

THE PLAN GOES AHEAD

'Something's wrong,' the major said lightly. Despite his words of warning he still bared his yellow teeth in a reckless smile. Bravado in the face of danger, that was the major's style. There were times when Sister Ironspeare found his military swagger tiresome. He hadn't lost any of his brio, even though half his face was now swathed in bandages following his encounter with Sam in the woods north of Stoneberry.

'Yes. Something's most definitely wrong,' the major continued. 'There should be a full-scale rescue operation going on in the village. The sky should be chock-a-block with helicopters. Ours is the only one. So much for getting lost in the crowd. We stick out like a sore thumb!'

He had to shout to make himself heard above the whirring of the blades.

'It doesn't matter! The plan goes ahead!' Sister Ironspeare shouted back, her cold, clear voice cutting through the noise of the helicopter.

'Well, blowing the sea wall has worked an absolute treat.' The major craned his neck to study the flooded landscape below. 'The headland is totally cut off. Even if the authorities do smell a rat they won't be able to get to Streaming Point, not for a while at least. And we won't have any nosy locals stumbling across us.'

'Just make sure you take out the power-station security guards with as little fuss as possible.'

'And what if they make a fight of it?'

'We must overwhelm them. Remember these are no ordinary guards. They're traitors to the Order. They were sent here to infiltrate the security on Streaming Point and keep the Book of the Last hidden. Since the death of their precious Master they've refused to hand over control to me. And yet I am the rightful leader of the Order. The book itself has prophesied it. They must die for their treachery.'

The major scanned the skies and his expression clouded. 'There's still no sign of the dragon, either. If his little pals took your bait they'll either be food for fishes by now, or sitting on a rooftop down there somewhere.'

'Should the beast dare to show its face, we'll kill it. It'll be no match for modern weaponry.'

The major shuddered and lifted a hand to his bandaged face. 'You didn't see it,' he said. Where was his swagger now?

'You're afraid of the dragon?' Sister Ironspeare's voice was filled with icy contempt.

'Of course not. I hate to leave a job half-done, that's all. Because of the wretched dragon spitting fire in my face, that lunatic Crisp managed to escape.'

'Don't worry, Major,' Sister Ironspeare said. 'The Book of the Last shall show us the way to hunt down all our enemies and rid ourselves of them once and for all, be they human or otherwise. Now order the rest of our men into the attack, and tell the pilot to bring us in to land.'

ULTIMATE HUNTERS

Fen flattened herself against the outer walls of the sealed building. She knew what was inside. She could taste its corrosive power through the thick concrete, and through the reinforced sides of the containment tank. Liquid nuclear waste. Acidic. Unstable. Deadly. Capable of contaminating an area hundreds of square kilometres in size.

There was a girl there, and a man too, close by. She felt his presence like something small, like an insect moving under bare feet. His brain squirmed. He was broken. Filled with disgust, Fen read his crumbling mind.

His name was Crisp. He believed himself to be a knight, but Fen could tell he was no such thing. He'd been a slave of the Order. Now they'd rejected him and condemned him to death. But still he came back to them.

And the girl? There was something unusual about her, about her memories, her emotions. But Fen decided to ignore both of them for the time being. There were others, true Knights of the Order, nearby. She could sense it.

The Order were the ultimate hunters. But Fen had escaped them. They didn't even know she existed. For a brief second she felt a surge of gratitude for the doomed Luhngdonese elders who'd returned to their ancestral home to seal her up at birth in her underground prison. Had they seen what the future held, that this moment would arrive, that the last pure-breed of the dragon line would be able to avenge them all? She would mete out vengeance, first on the Order of the Knights of the Pursuing Flame, then on the degenerate dragon-boy, a mockery of her heritage, and lastly, on humankind itself.

The lunatic Crisp, the half-breed dragon, and the others she could sense on the island, all of them could wait. None would stop her from releasing the contamination in the sealed building when the time came. But for the moment, she had another task to perform. Her mind cleared as she focused on the one activity that never failed to calm her. She would stalk the last Knights of the Order, and she would destroy them all.

WHERE SHE WOULD DROWN

An anguished yell tore itself from Sam's burning throat. A ball of fire arched over the shallows, landed in the water and boiled into a cloud of yellow steam.

His mind was out of joint. A stranger had broken in and robbed him of his senses. He was left half-blind, incapable of considered thought. Images burst across his vision without warning, obliterating the present. And the more he fought it, the worse it got.

Yet somehow he'd managed to locate Adda-Leigh. Out beyond the broken sea wall, he had felt her presence at last, beamed through the air like a radio signal. She was close at hand. She was travelling over deep water, heading for Streaming Point.

This was the place where she would drown. Sam had seen it in his nightmares. He saw it now in continuous snatches of broken visions. Adda-Leigh, struggling in the dark water. He had to get to her. He had to keep her safe.

He remembered throwing himself across the shattered concrete of the fallen wall and into the sea, speeding towards the boat he now knew Adda-Leigh was aboard. Thrashing his tail, clawing at the water with all four limbs, spinning like a torpedo, he hurtled towards his target. But, as he neared the headland, his mind was overpowered completely.

It was as if a serpent had been coiled up inside his skull, asleep, and that it had been there since the day he was born. Now that serpent was shifting, flexing its coils, awakening for the first time. The first shocking glimpse of the thing in the water had been the beginning. Now his head felt like it was about to explode.

He floundered. The tide took hold of him. He was close to land. He felt shingle beneath his body.

There was a sound. Banging and jolting. Dimly, he remembered the greenhouse in his grandmother's garden, the place where he'd been shot. He realised he could hear gunfire. Instinct told him to avoid the sound and he was too muddled to resist it. He swam out to deeper waters, and made landfall at the far end of Streaming Point.

And all the while the serpent twisted in his brain and an image danced before his eyes. A creature, scrambling over seaweed-encrusted rock. Large, impossibly powerful, all its senses developed beyond anything else on earth, able to read minds, able to glimpse the future. A creature of scale and claw, wing and tail. A creature like Sam. And it was here, on the headland. It was somewhere close by.

THE LIVING AND THE DYING

Georgette felt the sun on her face. The shallow water played over her naked feet. A breeze plucked at her hair, matted in strands across her nose and her mouth. Waves crashed on the shore.

She opened her eyes. She sat up, clutched at her stomach, bent over, retching and spitting out the bitter salt water. It was only then that the realisation struck her. She wasn't dead.

She crawled across sand and rock, through mounds of stinking seaweed to reach the cover of the gorse bushes that lined the shore. She followed an animal instinct that was telling her to hide, to keep out of sight until she could recover from her ordeal in the sea. She collapsed within the prickly shelter of the gorse.

She was glad of the warmth of the winter sun. It fell in golden patches on her sodden clothes, her frozen skin. Moments passed. The blood sang in her ears. Her heart was beating. She was alive.

A shout came from somewhere close by. A man was calling out urgently. His cry was suddenly cut off.

Careful to remain hidden, Georgette shifted her position so she could see what was happening on the beach. Her eyes widened. A group of men in black battledress were storming across the sand, heading inland. They'd arrived in kayaks, six or seven of the slender boats had been abandoned in the surf. They were met by men in dark-blue uniforms, who came running on to the beach.

At first, Georgette couldn't quite comprehend what was happening. Two of the men seemed to be locked in an embrace. Were they old friends? Both men collapsed to the ground, arms flailing. She heard their guttural cries of pain and fury. They were killing each other.

There was a sharp crack. Further up the beach, one of the men in blue seemed to be pointing with his arm outstretched towards a group of running figures. In his hand he held a gun. One of the running men fell face down in the sand and didn't get up. Georgette understood, then, that a pitched battle was taking place in front of her eyes.

SILENCERS

Sister Ironspeare had no military training and yet she wasn't afraid. She walked with the major through the battle zone, and didn't flinch at the sound of the gunfire. She behaved as if nothing could touch her because that was what she believed. Her faith was unshakeable. The Book of the Last would confirm what she already knew. She was destined for a place in history.

Glancing around at the dead men sprawled outside the power-station buildings, Sister Ironspeare frowned. 'The noise will have alerted the authorities. They'll know there's something happening at the power station.'

'Our weapons are all fitted with silencers,' the major said. A volley of shots echoed around the concrete buildings. The battle was still going on somewhere on the site. 'Unfortunately the guns the guards are using are not.'

'Has there been any contact with the official security forces?'

'We've intercepted no signals, no radio, no telephone, no communications of any sort.'

'Good. The guards may be traitors to the Order, but at least they haven't betrayed their oaths of secrecy and called in help from outside. If any of them surrender, spare their lives. They may prove willing to serve me in our glorious future.'

The major nodded. 'I'll pass the word round.'

'But still we must be quick. If the authorities send in the armed forces we'll be no match for them. Where is the folly?'

'This way. But keep your head down and stay close. Our men are still mopping up.'

Sister Ironspeare nodded. 'Gather the Order around the folly as soon as you can. We should all share in the moment we discover our final destiny!'

HEART HAMMER

Sam saw the first of the bodies lying in the surf. They were on the beach in front of the power station. The black combat gear of the men of the Order, and the dark-blue uniforms of the station security guards looked indistinguishable after a soaking in the sea. The two bodies rolled together in the breakers and the shingle. A red slick topped the water that sluiced around them.

Sam took the beach at a run, his wings spread out behind him, his clawed feet flicking up the sand. He reached a line of gorse bushes and plunged in amongst the prickly vegetation. This was where he found the third body. A wounded man had crawled into the shelter of the gorse, dragging his shattered leg behind him. A bullet had severed the main artery in his thigh. He'd bled to death, alone in the cavern of evergreen spines.

Sam made himself look at the dead man. One eye open, the other half closed. Mouth stretched in a grimace. Or a smile.

The dragon-boy realised how deeply in thrall he was to the turmoil in his mind. The muddled visions had cleared, temporarily at least, but he was still confused and disorientated. Normally the deaths of these men, occurring so close by, would have felt unbearably real to Sam. There would be no way he could have ignored, or failed to notice, what was happening. But today he'd been wallowing in the shallows, with his head full of images of a winged serpent, a dragon with the dark eyes of a girl, while just metres away these men had fought and died.

Sam kept his psychic powers firmly reined in. He couldn't risk another influx of blinding visions. Instead he relied on his senses, his speed, his strength. He hurtled forward, bursting into the open, clawing his way up the rocky slope that led away from the beach.

A gaping hole had been blown in the perimeter fence. Beneath a twisted and sagging post, another foot soldier of the Order lay dead. Several more bodies were sprawled in the dirt beneath the walls of the nearest of the power-station buildings. A detachment of raiders must have fought their way up from the sea, suffering heavy casualties as they pressed on.

But their sacrifice hadn't been in vain. A helicopter had landed on the flat roof of one of the larger buildings, probably bringing in a second wave of attackers. Sam could sense the heat still radiating from the helicopter engines. The pilot was seated at the controls, waiting for orders.

Down on the ground, Sam darted across the gap between the buildings, his wings beating silently. His claws skimmed the cement walkway but the helicopter pilot didn't so much as turn his head.

Up ahead there was a sealed building. Sam could feel his sixth sense twist within him. There was something lethal in this building, that much was clear. The radiation hazard symbols attached to the outer walls were enough to tell anyone that.

It was here that the security guards had made their last stand. Their bodies lay scattered beneath the bullet-scarred walls. The sea breeze tugged at their clothing and their hair, but Sam knew they would not rise again. He turned away, his heart hammering in his chest, his emotions churning at the horror of it all.

THE WAKE OF A MADMAN

Georgette lay in the gorse bushes, sodden and weary and chilled to the bone. She'd watched the battle move on. The men had fought their way up the beach and in amongst the power-station buildings that she could just glimpse through the spiky leaves of her hiding place, leaving their dead behind them. She had no real idea who they were, though she suspected the Order were involved. She just wanted to stay out of their way. So she lay in the gorse and tried to keep warm.

But when she heard the familiar sputter of an outboard motor she crawled back to the edge of the bushes and looked down at the beach. Crisp must have held back, watching the battle from a safe distance offshore, unnoticed by the combatants. Now he'd grounded his boat on the shingle and was marching Adda-Leigh up the beach at gunpoint. Georgette saw how her friend turned her face from the sight of the dead men lying sprawled around. Crisp however barely seemed to notice them at first, and when he did it was only to kick the arm of a sprawled corpse from out of his path.

As they grew closer to where she lay, Georgette could hear Crisp's harsh, broken voice droning on.

'Sister Ironspeare, she'll understand. She'll give me a reprieve when she sees that I've brought you here. You'll be the death of that dragon filth at last. He'll come for you, and we'll kill him. And that's what she wants. It's what we all want, in the Order. You know, I used to think it was your lot that were the problem. Foreigners, blacks, Asians, Chinese. But now I know better. It's the monsters, the dragons, the mutants, they're the real aliens. They're the real enemy.'

Adda-Leigh said nothing. She kept her eyes on the ground. She'd heard all this before.

Georgette wanted to rush out of the gorse bushes and attack Crisp. She wanted to strike him across the back of the neck with an iron bar. She wanted him dead. But there was no iron bar to hand, and even if there had been, she doubted she would have had the strength to lift it off the ground. All she could do was follow, dragging herself through the prickly foliage, hopelessly trailing along in the wake of this madman who, once again, had Adda-Leigh at his mercy.

FOLLY

Sam followed the scent of living humans and found the few survivors of the Order's assault team. They were grouped around the weathered remnants of a partially demolished tower. This was a building far older than the concrete blocks and chimneys that surrounded it. The power station had been built leaving this insignificant looking ruin in its midst.

Sam flattened himself on the ground and stilled his breathing, his blood flow and his heartbeat. If one of the men had looked round, they wouldn't have been able to see him.

Among the soldiers there was a man with half his face swathed in bandages, his hair, eyebrows and moustache singed and blackened. It was the major. Beside him stood the woman Sam had only previously seen in Crisp's memories and in the images that had been inadvertently left hovering in the ether of her headquarters. Sam was surprised by how ordinary Sister Ironspeare looked in reality. She stepped forward and addressed the men.

'You few —' she spread her arms, indicating them all '— you are the first of a new breed. Truly you are the Knights of the Order of the Pursuing Flame!'

The men gave a ragged cheer. Some of them were wounded and all of them looked exhausted. But still they turned their faces towards their leader and listened as she continued her speech.

'This place was once owned by ancestors of Bernard de Loup, the first Grand Master of our Order. This —' she gestured towards the ruined tower '— this folly was built to house the most precious treasure of all — the Book of the Last. And yet over the years successive Grand Masters failed to understand the significance of the book until it was forgotten. The people who placed it here didn't know what it was they were hiding. All they were told was that it must be kept hidden for ever. The perceived need to keep the book a secret led to this headland being sold to the authorities as a site for a nuclear power station. The owners of the land were of the Order. They knew how difficult this place would become to attack.

The guards who fought and died today didn't know

what it was they were defending. They were all misguided fools. What they strove to keep from us was no less than the ultimate truth. Our destiny is revealed in the book. Our promised reward. All will be made clear within its pages. Now we, the survivors of the Order, will come into our own. The last of the dragonfolk will be hunted down and killed. Our new purpose will be to follow the words of the book. And I, Sister Ironspeare, as leader of the Order, shall be the first to read our future history!'

Sister Ironspeare stood back and surveyed the men as they scurried around laying charges around the brickwork of the old tower, and the major radioed the helicopter pilot.

Watching all this, Sam began to feel increasingly uneasy. Something was about to happen and he needed to know what. But could he risk trying to worm his way into anyone's mind, with the dragon-girl somewhere in the vicinity? Sam feared for his sanity if the visions she generated took hold of him again. Perhaps now that the shock of discovering her existence was over he wouldn't be so badly affected. But he couldn't be sure. He just had to watch and wait.

The whirring of helicopter blades rent the air. Their pitch became ear-splitting as the flying machine lowered itself down over a square of open ground, beyond the remains of the old folly.

There was the muffled crump of an explosion and the ground heaved and shook. Smoke billowed from the base of the tower. The old brickwork fell away in a cloud of dust. Black-clad figures darted into the blasted ruin before the smoke had even cleared. Sister Ironspeare danced at their heels, almost unhinged with excitement, and then disappeared inside the remains of the folly.

Sam wasn't interested in whatever it was she was looking for. Just another of the endless prophecies that the Order seemed to thrive on. It filled him with disgust. Instead, he was looking at the helicopter. Something told him the pilot was not alone. And yet there'd been no one else with him when Sam had first seen the craft, perched on the rooftop. The major stopped in his tracks. He too had noticed something amiss.

Sam felt a jolt of horror run through him. Out of the helicopter stepped Crisp. He was pushing Adda-Leigh ahead of him. And he was pointing a pistol at the back of her head.

CIRCLE OF DEATH

Pushed off balance, Adda-Leigh stumbled and fell to her knees. When she looked up, a circle of men surrounded her. Filthy, with red-rimmed and staring eyes, some of them clutched bloody wounds; these were fighting men, with the light of battle still burning in their eyes.

In the power-station complex, Crisp had seen the helicopter on top of the building and had become very animated. With Adda-Leigh ahead of him, they'd climbed the fire escape to the roof. The pilot had already started the helicopter blades turning, so he'd heard nothing of their approach. And when Crisp shoved the pistol into his back, the man had made no attempt at resistance.

'I want to see Sister Ironspeare. Take me to her!'

The pilot had nodded his assent without question.

Now, kneeling in the dirt before a circle of vicious-eyed killers, Adda-Leigh realised Crisp had played into the major's hands. And she was just unlucky enough to be along for the ride.

'This is all wrong, Major!' The helicopter cut its engine and Crisp's shattered voice rang out. 'Our duty is to hunt the beast! To destroy the alien! But we've slaughtered each other, instead of the dragon! It's not too late. See? I have the girl. The girl that brings the dragon. It will be here soon!'

The major stepped forward. 'Well well,' he smiled, then winced. The injury to his face was clearly still causing him pain. 'It's you! Come to tell us how the Order should be run, have you, Mr Crisp?'

'You tried to kill me, Major. But I don't bear a grudge. I can see what that filthy dragon did to you. It burnt your face half off. How can you let it live?'

'Me, let it live? That dragon is as good as dead. I won't rest until I see the blighter's head mounted on the wall. But don't try to tell me you brought the girl. She was in Bernardscar all along. Sister Ironspeare saw to it. All you've done is confuse matters, just like you always do. It's time we put a stop to all that.'

Slowly, little by little, the major's men raised their weapons. Automatic machine-guns and pistols all pointing at Crisp and Adda-Leigh. She could only watch, frozen, as the scene unfolded. The major con-

tinued talking to Crisp with a mocking, deadly friend-
liness.

'You know, Crisp, perhaps I'm being a little too
harsh. Truth is, you're not half-bad. I mean, me, I was
born to come out on top. Right parents, right schools,
right contacts. Leader of men. It's in the blood. Bound
to succeed. But you? Working-class scum. Dragged up
in some ghastly tower block. Beaten like a dog all your
life but still you come crawling back, time and again.
Take now, for instance. After our little fracas in the
mental hospital, any sane man would have gone to
ground. But not you. Instead you come trailing out
here, all so you can get the chance to beg Sister Ironspeare to forgive you!'

'Where is she?' Crisp broke in. 'You have to tell her
I'm here. She understands! She —'

'She's got far more important things on her mind
right now, Crisp. I'm afraid you're history. Only the
fittest shall survive, and all that. Oh and, by the way,
thanks for returning my pistol. I was wondering where
that had got to.'

Adda-Leigh closed her eyes as she felt Crisp shove
the barrel of the gun against the back of her head. 'I'll
blow her brains out!' he said.

'What do I care?' said the major. 'If the dragon's
coming for her he'll come, whether she's alive or
dead. Open fire, chaps! Kill them both!'

HER SHIELD

All attempts at stealth abandoned, Sam gave a great cry. It emerged from his throat, not as sound but as a burst of roaring flame. He beat his wings and flailed his limbs, scattering pebbles and raising a great cloud of sand as he hurtled across the patch of open ground to get to Adda-Leigh.

The men of the Order turned, their faces frozen in expressions of shock and disbelief, mouths agape, eyes wide and staring. Then Sam was in amongst them, his tail thrashing wildly, gouts of fire bursting above their heads.

And all the while he was breathless with terror. Terrified in case they killed Adda-Leigh. And terrified in case, in the chaos of battle, he killed Adda-Leigh himself.

Then suddenly, it seemed, he was alone with her. She looked up at him, a great, scaled beast, rearing over her, flanks heaving, ash-flecked jaws reeking of fire. And he saw in her eyes, not the fear and revulsion he'd expected, but something else. Her face lit with recognition. Adda-Leigh smiled. 'Sam! Sam, it's you, boy! It's really you!'

He stared at her, transfixed by her eyes, her skin, her face. Then the first bullets ripped into him. A burst of gunfire caught him across the back, but his thickened hide withstood the impact. The bullets flattened against his scales. He coiled himself around Adda-Leigh as the bullets hammered into him. She huddled down, her hands over her ears. And she was unharmed. He was her shield.

Sam scooped up Adda-Leigh, sliced through the rope that bound her wrists with a delicate flick of the claw, and held her carefully. He raised his head and sent a spray of liquid flame scorching through the air in a fiery arc, forcing his attackers to dive for cover. All except one, the one person who had remained standing in the open throughout, who'd taken the brunt of the firing.

The ragged figure stood swaying before him, mortally injured. Crisp's body was riddled with bullet wounds, but he was still on his feet. Now he raised his pistol, held it in Sam's face and uttered his last words.

'Die, monster!' Crisp fired once, and then collapsed.

Sam blinked. He felt no pain, just a jolt that knocked his head back. Somehow, Crisp must have missed. Or the gun had jammed.

Sam had to tip his head to see properly, but there was no time to worry about that now. The dragon-boy sprang up, pushing off the ground, hard, with his back legs. He held Adda-Leigh gently but firmly, between his claws. With a beat of his wings he shot into the sky, leaving Crisp's body lying lifeless on the stony ground.

Sam thought he saw something flash past him, heading down as he flew up, but he was having trouble with his vision. He felt as if he'd got a large piece of grit in his left eye. It seemed to fill the eye completely. And now something was dripping down his face. Was he crying? He dropped height and landed on an outcrop of rock overlooking the power-station complex.

Hidden behind the rocks was a sandy hollow surrounded by a ring of stunted gorse bushes. Carefully, Sam laid Adda-Leigh down on the sand. She opened her eyes and looked at him. Her eyebrows puckered in alarm.

'Sam, you're hurt! It's your eye! You've been shot in the eye!'

FRESH FROM THE KILL

Georgette reached the vantage point of the ridge in time to see Sam, with Adda-Leigh held safely in his arms, stretch his wings and glide in to land on the outcrop of rocks. She could just glimpse the tops of the power station chimneys, over on the other side where the land dipped away. She'd kept to the cover of the gorse, climbing the high ground behind the buildings rather than following Crisp into the battle zone. She'd seen the helicopter drop down behind the ridge and had noted who'd been on board. She'd felt sick with fear for Adda-Leigh when she'd then heard repeated bursts of gunfire. Now, from beyond the rocks she heard the noise of the helicopter blades turning again.

She thought she saw something large burst out of the clouds and plummet to the ground. It disappeared behind the rocks. There was another rattle of small arms fire. And then screams. Terrible screams, brutally cut off.

With a great clatter of blades and a loud whine from its engines the helicopter rose jerkily from behind the rocks. It skimmed the ground and lurched upwards, passing just above them, the downdraught nearly throwing Georgette to the ground. The pilot and his passengers, a man with his face half covered in bandage, and a woman, a nun by the look of her clothing, were all looking back, craning their necks to watch for signs of pursuit, their eyes wide with fear. The helicopter gained height and headed out over the sea, hurtling along at a desperate speed.

Georgette saw a dark shadow pass over her head. Something following the helicopter. She stared, transfixed.

Its movements were leisurely, almost languid. Wings beat and tail flicked the air. It had scales like burnished gold. Claws extended, silver-blue, flecked here and there with splashes of red. Blood. It was a dragon. A dragon, fresh from the kill.

LAST LINES

Seated in the helicopter Sister Ironspeare clutched the book in her bony hands and hugged it to her body. The major had insisted they load the two chests full of treasure they'd also found in the folly. Bullion. Mere money. Trinkets of the Order. It excited the major but she had no interest in it. She had her book. The men had been bringing up the chests when the second dragon attacked. Only the major, the pilot and Sister Ironspeare herself had escaped.

The book's cover was plain. No gold inlay or precious stones, no pattern of any kind, just the blank surface of the leather binding. This pleased her. The Book of the Last wasn't gaudy or grand. It was the truth, unadorned and simple. She smiled. This was her moment.

'Did you see it?' The major's voice was laced with panic. 'Did you see that thing? Two of them! There's two of them!'

The pilot was in an even worse state than the major. He moaned, as if in agony.

'It killed them! It killed them all!'

'I can't believe there's two! How is it we didn't know this?'

'The blood! All that blood!'

But Sister Ironspeare wasn't listening. The clatter of the blades and the terrified jabbering of the two men faded into the background as, with trembling hands, she opened the Book of the Last. She turned the thick pages. They were made from vellum, the skin of calves, and each leaf was translucent. The book gave off a pungent smell. Sister Ironspeare breathed it in. Power. Knowledge. Destiny. The smell of glory.

She had no difficulty with the translation. She turned the pages, oblivious to anything but the words dancing before her eyes. And it was all there, just as she'd known it would be. The page that had been ripped out, the fragment she'd found that had led her to this final moment of triumph. And more. So much more.

'It's true! I am without doubt the prophesied leader of the Order. It's all here!' She spoke aloud, entranced by what she was reading. '" . . . And a Lady shall lead the Knights of the Order of the Pursuing Flame and the Knights shall arise and follow her and she shall be as the Empress of all the World to them . . .'"

She took no heed of the screams of terror from the pilot. She ignored the major, swivelling around in his seat, the skin of his face blanched the same colour as the bandage wrapped around his head. Whatever crisis they were facing she would let them deal with it. The major was a man of action, nothing was beyond him. They had the book and the prophecy didn't lie. What harm could they come to now?

She turned to the final pages, eager to read of how they would thwart this last despairing effort by the dragon-folk of Luhngdou, who had it seemed kept one of their number hidden for this futile roll of the dice. Her eyes scanned the concluding lines of the text. She translated as she read, and spoke the words aloud.

"'And the Knights of the Order, and their Lady, all shall perish. They shall be scattered over the face of the deep and the Order shall be no more. And the dragon shall slay the dragon. So it is written.'"

She closed the book quickly and placed her hands flat on the cover. 'Wait. This can't be right. We must have got the wrong book! Turn back, Major! Turn back at once!'

'Turn back? Are you mad?' The major practically

shouted into her face. 'Didn't you see it? Don't you know what's coming after us?' He was struggling to fit a new ammunition clip into his gun.

Sister Ironspeare looked out through the open door of the helicopter, back towards Streaming Point.

'There's nothing there, you fool! Turn back.'

A shadow fell across the helicopter. Something large was hovering just above them, easily keeping pace. The pilot let out a moan of pure terror. The major sat with his machine-gun held loosely in his hands, frozen, unable to act.

Sister Ironspeare jabbed the corner of the book into his back. He didn't respond. 'Do something, man!'

Galvanised into action, the major leant out of the helicopter and fired straight into the creature flying above them, not caring that the bullets struck the whirring blades. He fired until the clip was empty then he threw the gun out. It spun through the air, dropping down into the sea.

With shaking hands, the major grabbed a hand grenade from his rucksack. He pulled out the pin and grasped the explosive device firmly, holding down the trigger mechanism. When he let go, the grenade would explode.

'Well, what does it say?' The major nodded at the Book of the Last still on Sister Ironspeare's knees. 'How do we get out of this one?'

'The book is a lie!' Sister Ironspeare screamed. And she began tearing wildly at the pages, ripping the ancient vellum to flaking shreds.

FALLEN

Standing up on the ridge, Georgette watched the winged serpent close on its prey. It hovered above the whirring blades for a moment or two. There was a distant clatter of gunfire. It had no visible effect on the golden dragon. It fell on its prey in a frenzy of slashing claws and thrashing, reptilian tail. Metal screamed, and explosions ripped through the engines. Bent and buckled blades, torn fragments of cowling and broken skids fell from the stricken machine, sheared off in the dragon's furious attack. The great golden beast held the helicopter in a terrible embrace. Dragon and machine spun together, churning through the air. Torn pages of ancient manuscript, ivory statuettes and showers of precious stones and gold coins were flung out into the air as the dragon shook and tore and crushed the helicopter and the people inside it. At last, the remaining hulk of twisted metal was flung into the sea, discarded like an enormous piece of screwed-up litter. It fell into the water and disappeared beneath the waves, leaving nothing but a slick of spilled oil to mark where it sank.

Georgette swallowed. Her throat was dry and her eyes stung. The fumes of the downed helicopter still drifted on the air. Out at sea, the golden dragon banked and turned and came gliding across the surface of the ocean, heading back towards Streaming Point.

A MEETING IN THE FLOOD ZONE

Aaron stood knee deep in the stinking shallows and heaved at the grounded raft.

'If I catch something nasty from this water, it'll be all your fault.' He glared at Qua.

The old man folded his faded robes about him. 'Should you slip and fall, young Aaron, then try keeping your mouth closed as you go under.'

'That's nice, that is! I come all the way out here with you, floating on half a dozen planks of wood. And when the raft gets stuck in the mud, who has to get out and push? Muggins here! And what thanks do I get? Not a word. Just you, telling me to keep my mouth shut.' Aaron straightened with a groan. 'My back's killing me an' all.'

Qua smiled. 'You have admirable spirit. A most

admirable spirit. But you may rest now. Someone is coming. They will help us get closer to Streaming Point.'

'If it's the police they'll blooming arrest us! There's no way we're supposed to be out here in the flood zone.'

'The rains have stopped and the sea is receding,' Qua said, looking around at the waterlogged field. 'The tide pulls at the waters here. We are close to the ocean. I know we are near our journey's end.'

Aaron heard the sound of an oar in water. From behind a tall hedgerow, a long thin boat emerged. A man sat amidships, propelling the slender craft with a single paddle, dipping it on alternate sides. Despite the cold, he was dressed in a sleeveless sports vest. The muscles on his arms rippled as he drove the paddle into the water and then raised it, dripping, before plunging it back in on the other side. A steel-framed wheelchair had been folded up and was stowed in the bows, while in the stern of the canoe an old woman sat. She was as solid and imposing as a pile of weathered rock. The woman turned her head in the direction of the stranded raft and called out to her companion.

'Stop, Llewellyn. There's a couple here who could do with a lift, see?'

Aaron stared at the man in the boat. 'I don't believe it!' he said.

Qua nodded but remained silent. Aaron turned to him.

'You're not going to believe this, but I actually know that man in the canoe. It seems impossible, but it's true. He used to live near me in Marshside. Llew Evans. It's my mate's dad. It's Sam's dad. Sam's the . . .'

Qua held up his misshapen hand and Aaron fell silent.

'I know. This man's son is of the dragon-folk. And nothing, Aaron, is impossible.'

NO CHOICE

The dragon with the golden scales was, from nose to tail, around twice as large as Sam. Sinuous and serpentine, it spread its wings and hovered over the island, the daylight glittering on the gilded scales that covered its body. Its tail twisted, undulating in the air, and its crest of crimson spines rippled like antennae in the wind. There was a moment of stillness as Sam and Adda-Leigh stared up at the creature darkening the sky above them. Then the golden dragon began to scream.

Sam collapsed on the sand. He was aware of Adda-Leigh, crouched beside him, her hands clasped over her ears. All thought of his injured eye forgotten, Sam, too, clawed at the sides of his head in an effort to block out the terrible sound. But it was no good. The dragon's screams tore through the air and at the same time penetrated the minds of all those within range, boring into their thoughts and feelings like a psychic drill.

At last the screaming stopped and in the echoing silence that followed they heard the dragon speak. Except she wasn't speaking aloud. A youthful voice, harsh and cruel, was tapped directly into the mind, making it impossible to shut out. She spoke in English, with only the barest trace of an Oriental accent. It was clear that her intellect was as formidable as her physical powers.

'Hear me. I am Fen, last of the pure-bred dragon-folk. You are an abomination and I am here to destroy you and your human pets. Rise up from your sandpit and defend yourself!'

Sam groaned aloud and a lick of flame bubbled from between his clenched jaws.

'I see you flaunt your perversion. Breath of fire! You have acquired this grotesque trick, the spitting of flames. You've copied it from the twisted teachings of the West, just to pander to their prejudices. I know how dragons are viewed here. We are seen as vile, greedy brutes, hungry for gold and for flesh. And you can't forget that, can you? You writhe with self-loathing!

'You see, I know you. The power of my mind has read you from start to finish. You are the embodiment of our people's dissolution. Proof that the Luhngdonese have degenerated into a race of half-breeds. I thank the heavens you are the last of such creatures. Your death shall end our ancestors' shame.'

Sam struggled to lift his head. He twisted his neck to look up at Fen through his one good eye.

'Do not think to refuse this combat. I have no interest in peace. This world is nothing to me. I can read it all. I know every thought, every language, every philosophy of humankind, and all of it disgusts me. The skies here are too low and the earth too cluttered for me to ever find rest. So do not turn your cheek. You have no choice but to fight. And know this. When you are slain, I shall tear down the buildings on this island. I shall rip open the tanks of contaminant, and release the deadly waste into the sea. Then I shall drink deep of it, take the poison into my lungs and spread my vapour about the heavens until phlegm-coloured clouds choke the sun and stifle the moon. Then a great deluge shall fall. And the earth shall drown in poison. So you see, you have no choice. No choice at all.'

SPEECH WITHOUT SOUND

Fen looked down at the half-breed dragon-boy squirming in the sand beneath her. He was barely able to look at her, twitching and grovelling on the ground as if she had already defeated him, and he was flinching in craven anticipation of the *coup de grâce*.

'I see you need proof of my ability to carry out my threats.' Fen had no intention of allowing this cowardly animal a quick and merciful end. She gave a flick of her tail and beat her wings hard. She went darting down between the power-station chimneys, heading for the sealed building and the tanks of radioactive waste. She knew he would follow.

She swept down upon the windowless building, its white walls weathered by countless island storms, and landed on top of it. She began pounding the concrete roof with her tail. Again and again. She slammed and hammered relentlessly until she could feel the concrete begin to weaken beneath her.

Then the dragon-boy arrived, plummeting awkwardly out of the sky like a moth burnt in a candle flame. He crouched on the edge of the roof, breathing hard. Flames flickered around his blackened lips. One eye was terribly injured, weeping blood and optic fluid from an empty socket. He turned his head to look at her.

Then they both heard the call. A human voice, spoken telepathically. Someone had learnt the skill of speech without sound. This was the voice of a person who knew the dragon-folk better than anyone else alive. Fen recognised the voice instantly.

'Qua! It is Qua! So. He has found me. Sneaked up on me. Kept his presence hidden, somehow, the old devil! Very well. Then he shall witness my finest hour!'

The dragon-boy moved towards her, his one eye blinking stupidly.

'We are yet to begin, half-breed! But you are not to escape me now.' Fen shot out a clawed hand and seized Sam by the neck. Dragging him with her, she rose into the air and turned towards the mainland.

ON THE STRANDED DUNE

Qua was standing on the edge of the water, the waves breaking over his feet, soaking the hem of his robes. His eyes were closed and his arms outstretched. His lips moved but he was making no sound that Aaron could detect.

Llew was muttering curses, stubbornly trying to manoeuvre his wheelchair in the damp sand. Aaron had helped him climb out of the canoe and unfold the chair, but he'd received nothing but angry looks by way of thanks. When Llew did speak it was to deliver some angry accusations. 'Why didn't you shout a warning? You must have seen that fence post in the water, you dozy oaf!'

The old Welsh woman was seated among the waving grasses on top of the dune. She'd wrapped her shawl about her shoulders and seemed to be waiting patiently to see what would happen. 'Leave the boy alone, Llewellyn!' she called out. 'He's a friend of Sam's, isn't he? It wasn't his fault the canoe's been sunk. It's lucky we managed to reach this dune, that's what I say. Mister Qua says we're near enough.'

'Near enough for what, I'd like to know, Mother?' Llew glared at the old man standing in the surf. 'It's my son I need to see, not some old lunatic. That's why we've come all this way, isn't it? What's Qua doing down there anyway?'

Aaron sighed. 'I've given up trying to figure him out. He never tells me anything.'

'If I'd wanted your opinion I'd have asked for it!' Llew's eyes flashed angrily.

Aaron looked away. 'Pardon me for breathing!' he muttered.

He was cold and he was hungry and he didn't know what was going on. He and Qua had crossed the last of the flooded fields with Llew and his mother, in their canoe. It seemed extraordinary that an old woman and a man in a wheelchair had got all the way out to this devastated coast, but then, Aaron reasoned, he and Qua had managed it. Llew seemed to be bent on some kind of reconciliation with Sam. That was probably well overdue. Sam had never got on well with his father.

The journey had come to an abrupt end. Aaron had felt a sudden jolt as the sunken fence post tore through the wooden hull. They'd just made it to the sand dune before the inrushing water swamped the canoe completely. Now he was here, stranded in the middle of a flood, with two crazy old people and a paraplegic ex-fireman with a permanent scowl on his face. He didn't know how he was going to get back home, or see his family again. Clamping his hands under his armpits to try to keep them warm, Aaron climbed up the shifting sands to the top of the dune.

He saw the old woman look up. Her eyes widened and she lifted a hand to point wordlessly out to sea. Swooping low over the waves, their wings beating, necks outstretched, tails trailing behind them, flew two huge creatures. The leading beast was the larger of the two. It was gold and crimson in colour. It had the smaller creature in some kind of hold, clasping its rust-orange and slate-blue neck in a fearsome grip. The two dragons were heading straight for the sand dune.

THE BAMBOO PENDANT

Fen flew arrow straight, dragging Sam behind her. They reached the stranded sand dune in less than a minute. Sam was thrown unceremoniously into the shallows. He floundered there, spluttering and choking.

When he looked up he saw an old man standing at the water's edge. This was the man who had called Fen to him with his mind, Sam was sure of it. Behind him were a small group of people. They were as familiar to Sam as they were unexpected.

Sam's eyesight was losing clarity. But he had no trouble recognising his grandmother and his father and Aaron. But who was the fifth figure, standing apart from the rest, her black hair blowing in the wind? No. Must have been a trick of his damaged sight. There were only four.

Sam scrambled on to the sloping sands of the dune and coiled himself into a circle, head raised in a defensive posture. Despite the presence of the terrifying golden dragon, he was now among friends and family and he was determined to draw strength from the presence of some of them, at least. He saw Grandma Evans smile but he wouldn't look at his father. And there was Aaron. It was good to see him. Now he'd turned pale and was struggling to speak. It had been a while since he'd last seen Sam.

'You're . . . you *are* Sam, aren't you?'

Sam tipped his head to look at his old schoolfriend.

'Sam! It's me, mate. Aaron!'

Sam let his words fall into Aaron's mind. *Yes, Aaron. I know. It's me that's changed, remember? You look just the same.*

Aaron gawped at Sam. 'What happened to your eye?'

'Never mind that.' Sam turned to look at the old man. *'Who is he?'*

'I am Qua,' the old man replied for himself. He'd obviously been able to hear Sam's thoughts via Aaron's mind. 'I am the last human survivor of the people of Luhngdou. You and Fen are my only relatives. Your friends and your family have come here, Sam, whether they realise it or not, because a part of them knew that you would need their support, here and now, at this meeting place.'

Qua turned to Fen. She was rearing over the dune, held upright by the beating of her wings, her tail whisking the waves that rolled against the sand.

'And I came here because of you, Fen,' he said.

The dragon bent her neck and lowered her head, her blazing eyes fixed on the old man.

'Tell me why I shouldn't kill you?'

Qua smiled, but there was sorrow in his eyes. 'You may destroy me whenever you choose to. And yet there is so much I could teach you, about yourself, about the dragon-folk, about the world.'

'You? Teach me? Ha!' The golden dragon let out a vicious squawk of laughter. *'I've no interest in the world. The world disgusts me! And I've no interest in you, Qua. All that you know, I know. I read your mind, remember? You can teach me nothing!'*

'How is it, then, that I have come so close to you without you sensing my approach? I have managed to mask my mind from you all this time, Fen. There is much that you haven't been able to see. I left the caverns of Luhngdou a different man from when I arrived. How else could I have survived? Living with you for so long gave me more power than I realised. I followed you here because I knew that this was where we would meet. And I found that there was another like you. Not a pure-breed perhaps, but one of the dragon-folk nonetheless, going through the same changes, the same traumas as you. And here, in this place, you have found each other.'

'*I am here to slaughter this mutant thing! The only reason for our meeting is so that he shall die!*'

'It doesn't have to be that way. Please, Fen. Put aside your anger. The dragon-folk were never the enemies of humankind. On Luhngdou, the dragons offered strength, salvation and protection.'

'*And how did the rest of humankind repay us? By coming to our island and slaughtering our people! You're a fool, old man!*' Fen's voice scoffed. '*You should have stayed buried in the earth where I left you. You can change nothing!*'

Fen whipped her tail through the shallows, spraying Qua with seawater.

'*After I've killed this . . . monstrosity,*' she said glaring at Sam, '*I shall release the poison rain. I shall flood the lands of the earth with death.*'

'I see.' Qua turned back to Sam. 'And what of you, Sam? What will you do?'

'*I don't want to fight.*' Sam lowered his head.

'I did not ask what you wanted. Do you know what will happen if Fen is allowed to realise her threat?'

'*Yes.*' Sam remembered doing a school project on the Cold War. He'd read up on the threat of nuclear war and the effects of radiation poisoning. It was the sort of information that had stuck, burned into his mind, though he would much rather have forgotten it. *'Anyone close to the site when the waste is released will get sick. Nausea, vomiting, diarrhoea, headache, sores on the mouth and throat, hair loss, inflamed heart, bleeding under the skin . . . Most will be dead within a few weeks. For those who survive, and for those further away, the risks will be more long term, but just as deadly. The world can expect a huge increase in terminal cancers, birth deformities in humans and animals, crops will be . . . '*

'Enough!' Qua held up one of his ruined hands. 'Fen. I beg you, one last time. Instead of violence, choose serenity. Instead of wild destruction, choose stillness and calm.'

'Beg all you wish, but you'll get no charity from me.'

Qua sighed. 'Even as a child, before the changes took hold of you, you were a creature of immense power. I made a terrible mistake. I hoped to keep all knowledge of what you are, what you're capable of, hidden from you. I hoped that if I told you nothing – that you might be content to remain below ground. Safe – who knows? Perhaps you would have survived there for ever. You have no need of food to eat or air to breathe. The rules of the world do not apply to such as you. You live by other rules. Rules that lie far beyond the physical realm. Why deal in death, when you might live for ever? Why destroy, when you could build wonders?'

'Do not waste your breath, Qua. I am not listening.'

Qua lowered his head. 'I know now that I have failed in my guardianship.' His voice was racked with sorrow. 'Forgive me.'

The old man reached for the cord around his neck, twisting the bamboo pendant with a movement far quicker than seemed possible, and pulling something from inside it. Immediately, he struck out, stabbing wildly at the dragon's muzzle. In his hand he held a long needle, viciously sharp, the point tipped with a dark substance.

But although Qua was quick, Fen was quicker still. She leapt backwards, out of his reach, and, in one swift and sinuous movement, she brought her tail around from behind her and lashed at Qua. Something flew though the air and dropped into the sea. It took a moment for Sam to realise that it had been Qua's severed hand, still clutching the deadly needle. The old man dropped to his knees, his blood darkening the sand.

'You dare try to poison me? To deceive me?' Fen gave a shriek of fury. 'You shall die slowly, old man, mired in your own gore. Stay here. The waste I shall release from the buildings on the headland will claim your life. But first you shall see me rid the world of the half-breed!'

ANGELS AND REPTILES

Adda-Leigh climbed unsteadily to her feet. She made her way out of the cover of the gorse bushes. Sam had gone, dragged away, lost. He would survive, she was sure of it. But still, Adda-Leigh felt cold and afraid and horribly alone. She didn't want to go back to the power station. There were dead bodies everywhere. So she stumbled down a trail leading to the beach and there was Georgette, limping along on her bare feet.

'You're alive!'

'You're alive too!'

Adda-Leigh screamed and whooped and threw her arms around Georgette's neck and the two girls danced in delight.

'What now?' Georgette said, when they'd both calmed down.

'I'm sick of waiting around to get rescued.' Adda-Leigh slapped her hands together. 'Let's get out of here!'

Georgette frowned. 'Did you see the other dragon? Did you hear its . . . voice?'

Adda-Leigh shuddered. 'I heard it.'

'Then is there any point? I mean, if that . . . thing empties the nuclear waste into the sea . . .'

'We're not giving up, Georgette. When have we ever just sat down and waited to die? Come on, let's find Crisp's boat.'

'Crisp. Is he . . . ?'

Adda-Leigh grimaced. 'I don't want to think about him. Not now. He's not going to harm us any more, that's all that matters.'

'When the tide first washed me up here, I thought I was dead.'

'Dead? Well you don't look much like an angel to me, girl!'

'Looks aren't everything, Addy. After all, your boyfriend's a giant reptile.'

'Yeah,' Adda-Leigh grinned. 'He is, isn't he?'

IN WATER AND IN FIRE

Fen began the fight by holding herself in check. She had no doubt that she was going to win, so she decided to allow Sam to retain some dignity throughout the initial bout. Where was the fun in an easy victory?

But he was a pitiful creature. Confused, wounded, half-sighted and stumbling, it was as if he were already dead. He just hadn't realised it yet.

The two dragons plunged below the surface of the sea and were soon stalking each other through the murky water. Sam swam ahead, leading her into the shallows, back towards the flooded village. She humoured him, and followed.

Out in the air again, they dodged around the ruins of the sea wall. Fen made a few flying feints, slashing at Sam with her claws, but not making any contact. Not yet.

There were shouts and startled yells. A boat full of rescue workers, together with some victims of the flood wrapped in blankets, stared up in horror at the two impossible creatures that had emerged from the sea.

Sam leapt from the broken wall and dived beneath the filthy waters of the flooded, rubbish-choked streets of Bernardscar. Fen shrugged off the instinct to remain hidden from humans and followed him. If they wanted to stare, then let them stare. They'd soon know who she was and what she was capable of, when she finished the demolition job at the power station.

Minutes later she had Sam cornered in the water-filled frontage of the village shop. There was a police-man in a rowing boat stationed outside the flooded building. He watched, slack-jawed with astonishment, as Sam and Fen surfaced, one either side of him. Then he dropped his oars and covered his face with his hands. Sam dived again and pushed himself through the doorway of the shop. The bell jangled under the water.

Listening outside, Fen heard Sam drag himself out of the water and up to the top of the stairs. His breath came in gulps. He was tiring already.

She shook the drops from her wings. Why bother to keep silent? If he guessed her next move it would only make things more interesting. She launched herself out of the water, like a missile fired from a submarine, described a delicate arc in mid-air and plunged in through the first-floor windows of the flat above the shop. Glass, wood and brickwork all shattered or shifted as she forced her way inside.

Charging into the hall, tearing the door off its hinges as she went, she was just in time to see Sam disappear downstairs and back beneath the waters of the flooded shop. Dozens and dozens of bags of crisps, in assorted flavours, bobbed on the surface, obscuring the murky depths. But Fen heard the muffled jangling of the shop bell sounding once more, as Sam passed out through the door to the street.

The policeman was still sitting in his boat with his hands in front of his eyes when Fen surged past him, hot on Sam's trail.

She ran the dragon-boy to ground again at the petrol station. This was up the road, on higher ground. The flood was no more than a metre deep here. The building had been evacuated nonetheless and a guard consisting of a fireman and a special constable had been posted outside, perhaps to deter looters. When they'd seen Sam and Fen approaching the two men had abandoned their rubber dinghy, leaping into the filthy water and splashing away in a feverish panic to escape.

Now Sam was trying to hide from her. A pointless exercise. If she wanted, Fen knew she could seize his mind with her own, and force him to show himself, make him submit through the power of her will alone. But where was the fun in that? She preferred to keep the fight physical, for now, at least.

Sam came bursting out from behind the unleaded pumps in a great churning swell of petrol-topped water. Fen glared at him. He kept looking away to his left, craning his head, as if to see something or someone standing there, watching them.

'Is this a puerile attempt to trick me?'

'I thought I saw someone . . . there was . . . I don't know . . . a woman?'

Fen laughed out loud. *'You're losing your wits as well as your eyesight. But you've more suffering to come. You'll pay for all that the humans have done to us.'*

'Some humans are good.' Sam shook his head compulsively and squinted at her through his one good eye. *'They've helped me, protected our kind, died for us, even.'*

'They all wanted something! Power, knowledge, mastery. They are parasites. All of them. After I've killed you, they shall perish too.'

'No!' Sam opened his jaws wide and let out a furious roar. Tongues of flame shot from his mouth. He churned the standing water into waves, lashing the surface with his tail, spraying every corner of the petrol station with wreaths of fire.

The explosion that ripped through the underground

tanks sent plumes of water boiling fifty metres into the air. Instantly, the flooded garage forecourt became a raging inferno.

THROUGH THE ELEMENTS

Sam was thrown across the road by the force of the blast. He landed with a great hiss of steam in the water-filled front garden of an evacuated cottage. By the submerged wall, the bare branches of a mountain ash tree reached out of the flood like the hand of a drowning man. Sam peered around the slender trunk, his body submerged, his neck and head jutting from the water. The scales on his body were scorched and soot-stained but the explosion hadn't hurt him. He instinctively knew that his hide could withstand far greater temperatures and he was sure that Fen's could too. But there was just a chance some razor-sharp fragment of debris had been blown into her, piercing some vulnerable patch of skin. Or maybe a section of the blazing roof had collapsed and pinioned her to the ground. There was just a slender chance that she might have been stopped.

Cautiously Sam swam out in front of the blazing garage. The raging fire licked at the sky and a billowing plume of black smoke rose in a thick column over-head. He craned his neck, turning his face this way and that. He blinked his good eye. The hot air shivered like a mirage. Nothing moved except the leaping flames and the drifting smoke.

Sam let out a sigh of relief. He relaxed his limbs and let himself drift, floating on the shallow floodwater. He could hardly believe it had been so easy to defeat the fearsome Fen.

Then a furious scream rent the air and a sinuous shape came hurtling out of the black smoke. It was her, the scales along her back a little tarnished but otherwise unharmed. She slashed at his muzzle with her claws as she swept over him. Sam dived.

He swam away, down through the submerged back gardens of the village houses and out into the flooded meadow beyond. There was no sign of the rescue teams. Everyone who could had fled the village. Those few who couldn't escape had shut themselves in their upstairs rooms and were desperately trying to think of some explanation for the beasts they could see battling in the flooded streets.

The waters had already begun to recede. The fields

beyond the meadow were dotted with pools and the ground was heavy with slime. Sam scrambled out of the sodden pasture, his body spattered with wet mud. He beat his wings and climbed skyward. With another wild scream, Fen came after him.

'*You cannot escape me! In fire, in water, on the earth or in the air, I shall run you down!*' Sam heard her harsh voice rasping inside his head. He knew then that he was afraid of her. Very afraid. He beat his wings with frenzied speed and headed up into the open sky.

Higher and higher he flew. The air became thin. Pain wracked his wings, his shoulders, his back as he climbed ever higher. But nothing could slow his flight unless Fen caught up with him.

Then a voice broke into his thoughts. It was Fen. She was trying to brainwash him.

'*Stop. Turn back. You must obey me. This fight is over. Surrender yourself. Obey me.*'

The words repeated themselves over and over, seeming to swell and echo around his head until he couldn't tell if they were his own thoughts or those of another. The words spoke the truth. The fight was over. He was beaten. He had to turn back.

But he didn't. The fear that twisted inside his guts wouldn't let him turn, wouldn't even allow him to slow down. Adda-Leigh was back there in Bernardscar. So was his gran, his dad, his best friend. He had to lead Fen away from them. He would not turn. The voice grew shrill, desperate.

'Turn back! Obey! You are beaten! Surrender, I command it!'

Sam wouldn't listen. The voice dwindled and faded. He realised then, to his great surprise, that his will was actually stronger than Fen's. She was the more powerful dragon, there was no doubt of that. But she couldn't control him. He was still free. Free to run from her. Free to devise a plan that she wouldn't be able to anticipate. He knew he had to lead her further away from Streaming Point, to get her as far away as possible from the power station, and all the people he cared about. He only hoped his strength would hold out.

Sam didn't dare look around. He could sense that she was gaining on him. His chest was heaving with effort and all his muscles burned with the torment of maintaining this savage velocity. And still Sam rocketed onwards.

He became dimly aware that he was entering a new state, a state of the extreme. Never before had he come anywhere near testing the upper limits of his altered body's abilities. Now, he realised, he would not only discover those limits, but also journey to some place far beyond them.

The sky was darkening. Stars winked through the

high vapour. Sam had reached the inner edge of the planet's atmosphere. Ahead of him lay heat as he had never known it before, cold far deeper than anything possible on earth. He didn't allow himself to slacken his pace, not even for an instant. He knew now, that no matter how far he went it wouldn't be far enough to escape the claws of the golden dragon. He would have to turn and make his stand, somewhere far, far above the earth. But he must choose his spot well. He had to lead her to the very limits of the earth's influence, where gravity gave way to the endless reaches of space. Then, and only then, would he turn and fight. And when that happened their fate would be sealed. Only one of them would ever return.

DEAD HAND

Two air-force jets swept silently over the flood zone. It was only after they had passed that the sound of their engines could be heard, rolling like thunder across the bay.

Beyond the outskirts of the village of Bernardscar, at the limits of the waterlogged fields, there were chaotic scenes. Bewildered rescue teams and evacuees clogged the roads. Army jeeps and personnel carriers tried to ferry squads of soldiers against a tide of men, women and children, many of them filthy, bedraggled and wide-eyed with shock.

Out on the open water, a navy launch plucked a dozen men from the sea. They were the coastguard command crew, whose last radio message had ordered the rescue operation to be put on hold. None of them had any memory of why they'd sent the message and how their boat had come to sink under them.

The response of the authorities to what they were already referring to as 'the Benardscar incident' was shifting in its nature, from a rescue mission to a military operation. Gunfire had been heard from the area of the old nuclear power station. And people had seen things they couldn't properly explain. At all levels of command, utter confusion reigned. As a result those at the sharp end, down on the ground or on the water, proceeded with extreme caution. An exclusion zone was set up around Bernardscar and Streaming Point, but as yet, neither the army nor the navy was willing to send their men in. Not before they knew what they were up against. There were some wild stories flying around.

Deep beneath the waves, the wreckage of a helicopter lay scattered over the seabed. The dead bodies of the last three members of the Order were trapped in the largest section of the downed machine. Their long war had come to an end. They were at peace now. And yet one of the dead still had the power of destruction, literally in his hands. The major still held the unexploded grenade in his rigid grasp.

The deep-sea current plucked at his tattered battle-dress. Behind him, the ruptured fuel tanks of the helicopter leaked oil into the water. Slowly, the grenade began to slip out of the dead man's hand.

SWALLOWED UP

Georgette and Adda-Leigh struggled to drag the boat out beyond the breakers. It hadn't been hard to find. Crisp had left it beached on the shingle.

At last, with the boat lolling on the swell, they heaved themselves up over the side. As they drifted out from the shore, they pushed through banks of floating rubbish washed from the flooded village. A red bucket banged against the prow. A deflated football bobbed in their wake. Plastic bags spread across the surface like diseased water lilies. They sat with the seawater dripping from their sodden jeans, shivering with cold while a strong current carried them out into deep water.

'Should we start the motor?' Georgette looked at Adda-Leigh. 'Do you know how it works?'

'Not sure. Is there a button with "Start" written on it?'

'Funny. I think you pull some sort of cord thing. Do you remember how Crisp worked it?'

'Sorry, I was a bit distracted by the gun in his hand.'

They were midway between the island and the mainland. The wind picked up and the air grew colder still. It was late afternoon. Evening would follow soon.

'I don't want to be out here when it gets dark,' said Adda-Leigh. 'Let's have another look at this motor.'

As she moved towards the stern a deep and ominous boom sounded from somewhere beneath the waves. An underwater explosion.

Within seconds there was a great stirring of the surface. Oil-covered debris came bubbling up, bursting into flames as the fragments reached the air. The boat lurched, tipped by the heaving swell the explosion had whipped up. Adda-Leigh gave a squawk of alarm and pitched forward. She was thrown headlong over the side and dropped like a stone into the heaving sea. As she fell she struck her head, with a sickening thud, against the cowling of the outboard motor.

Georgette gazed stupidly at the waves for a moment. Then she looked wildly around the boat, searching for a lifeline, something, anything, to throw over the side for her friend to cling on to. She remembered the rope

Crisp had made her tie Adda-Leigh's wrists with. There was no sign of it now.

She leant over the side and dragged her hands through the water, trying desperately to paddle the boat back to where Adda-Leigh had fallen in. But the waves seemed to be pushing the boat further and further away.

'Addy!' she screamed.

There was no sign of her. The sea had swallowed her up.

THE PLACE

A shower of tiny meteors blazed in the darkness. A great curtain of light hung, shimmering with colours that flickered and pulsed, through acid yellow and emerald green to azure blue, magenta and deep crimson.

Fen wouldn't give up now. The dragon-boy had surprised her. His flight had filled her with outrage. How dare he run away? But the speed he'd achieved had come as a shock. And when he'd resisted her attempt at mind control she'd started to feel a tinge of concern.

So she was no longer holding herself back. She'd given him far too much leeway already. He'd evaded her for too long. She was beginning to wonder if she'd made a mistake in following him this far, but there was no turning back.

He was still ahead of her, his body glowing like a burning coal from the intense heat as he streaked through the darkness and on into the drifting clouds of pulsating light. She had no choice but to follow.

At last, far beyond the aurora, Sam slowed and turned and prepared to make his final stand. The pull of the earth's gravity, which had held them fast and spun them into a slow but secure orbit, was barely noticeable here. Fen bared her teeth in an exultant snarl and moved in for the kill.

To her annoyance, the dragon-boy wasn't even watching her approach. He should have been gibbering with fear, or begging her for mercy. Instead he just floated there, in the weightless void. His one good eye rolled in his head and he gazed around as if he had no idea where he was. Had he lost his mind completely?

'So. This is where it all changes.' She heard his voice, his words forming in her head. 'This is the way it goes. Funny, I never thought about it until now. Until the end.'

'You're babbling again.' Fen shot back her reply. 'Now be still and let me put you out of your misery.'

'No,' he said. 'Ever since I became what I am, I've been hunted down time and again and made to fight, whether I wanted to or not. People have been hurt because of me, and people have died. It's time that it was stopped. All of it.'

Fen struck at him with her claws but there was little

force in the blow. A shower of sparks flew from Sam's scales and sailed earthwards, shimmering like glow-worms. Fen felt a wave of exhaustion break over her. Had she come too far?

Sam spoke again. *'We're impossible creatures, Fen. We don't obey the rules of nature. We don't belong on the earth, I see that now.'*

'Talk all you want. The silence of death awaits you!'

Fen flexed her tail and turned in the airless void. She felt a great weakness take hold of her, but she shook off the feeling and summoned one last effort. She bared her glistening teeth but her battle scream was stifled by the soundless reaches of space.

Fen swept down upon her enemy, saw him writhe and spin, the stars forming a brilliant halo behind his head. At the last moment, he slipped away from her flailing claws and she shot past him, out of control, turning, spinning, too far, too far!

She knew then with a sudden shocking certainty that she'd been defeated. The mutant, the half-breed, the human-lover, he had beaten her. All through his headlong flight, which Fen had taken for mere cowardice, he'd actually been planning this final reversal. And he'd shielded these thoughts from her as they formed in his mind. She'd been caught out. It was over. She was drifting, falling, rolling over and over, slipping away, lost in the wake of the world. Here, the last vestiges of gravity could no more hold her mass than a spider's web could have carried her weight down on earth. She would never see the sky again. Now she was a part of it.

'Fen! Fen, I'm sorry.' The dragon-boy's voice chimed inside her head.

She looked at her scorched and buckling scales and knew she didn't have long left.

'What have you done? You've destroyed me!'

'I just did what I had to do. I had no choice, remember?'

Fen laughed then. Suddenly it all seemed to make sense. A cloud of light was blossoming in her mind, filling her thoughts with abstract images. Her rage lifted. She'd been defeated in battle by an inferior, she was drifting into deep space with no way of returning, but somehow she no longer cared. A strange excitement took hold of her.

'Wait! This is extraordinary. Perhaps you're right . . . perhaps I didn't belong down there, on the planet. Maybe there is a place. Somewhere. Another place. Wait a moment. Look there. Look! Oh look!'

She saw the earth turning, trailing sparkling motes of atmosphere behind it, kissed by solar wind and warmed by the radiance of the sun. She opened her eyes and mouth wider and wider. She wanted to drink it all in. The vastness. The unending. The infinite wonder. She screamed silently into the darkness, but this time it was a scream of pure delight. The dragon-boy was right. She didn't want the earth. This was the place. At last, this was the place.

ICARUS FALLING

An invisible thread still bound Sam to the earth. Something that stopped him following Fen into the emptiness of space. And even though he had come too far, suffered too much to ever make it back unscathed, he still turned and faced his home planet. And he swam, through waves of crushing cold, on into the blazing heat of the radiation belt. His skin, his muscle and bone, the blood in his veins, all boiled and calcified and dried and turned to crumbling dust and yet he held together and would not die. He had to keep going. He had to return, to get home.

It was the old nightmare back again, driving him on, keeping him focused on one final task. The dreaded vision had appeared the moment Fen vanished into the swallowing vastness of space. The images flickered through his mind and kept him moving, dropping down through layers of atmosphere towards the surface of the earth. Once again he saw Adda-Leigh suffocating, choking, dying in front of his eyes. She was under the water, drowning, down there on the blue planet.

Sam kicked furiously at the thickening air, thrashed his limbs, his tail, beat his wings to speed his tumultuous descent. He had to get to her. Had to pull her from the dark water before it was too late.

Flames flickered over the surface of his body. A tail of light trailed behind him like a shooting star. He blazed across the sky. And like Icarus burning, he plunged down and down and fell into the sea.

WEIGHTLESS

On the sand dune, Aaron looked out to sea. 'Where's all the rescue ships? Helicopters? Anything?'

All he could see was one little boat way out in the bay. In the fading light it was impossible to say who was on board or what they were doing.

Llew and Grandma Evans had been tending to Qua's wound. Aaron had splashed around in the shallows, looking for the old man's severed hand, but without success. There was no chance of a hospital being able to reattach it now.

'Maybe a big old lobster took it,' Aaron said. He was talking to fill the silence. Anything was better than the silence. Secretly, he was glad he hadn't found the hand. He didn't think he'd have been able to pick it up without being sick.

There was a sudden flash of light in the darkening sky and a blazing star fell like a streak of lightning. Something plunged into the water.

'A meteor!' Aaron said. 'Did you see it? Who saw it?'

Qua spoke softly, through his pain. 'It is Sam. He has returned. Now the sea must claim him.'

Llew peeled off his vest. 'Aaron!' he called. 'Drag me down to the water!'

'Llewellyn Evans!' The old woman turned her great stony head towards her son.

Llew didn't wait to hear what she had to say. 'Qua's bleeding is under control. He'll be all right, you know what you're doing. I have to go out there, Mam. Don't try to stop me. This is why we came, isn't it? I know I've been a fool. A coward and a fool. I'm afraid I'm going to outlive all the people I love. That may well be so, I can't say I don't deserve it. But I'm not going to let my Sam be taken by the sea, without at least trying to lend him a hand.'

Aaron grunted with exertion, heaving the wheel-chair-bound man into the waves.

'Swim, Llewellyn!' the old woman said at last. 'Go see your boy again, and set things right this time! I don't think you'll get another chance.'

Llew slipped awkwardly into the water. But once in amongst the surf he struck out with his powerful arms and pulled himself forwards, cutting through the waves, his paralysed legs stretched out behind him, weightless in the water. He made for the place where the star had fallen. Out in the bay where the little boat was drifting.

BEATING HEARTS

Adda-Leigh gazed sightless at the surface of the water far above. Her braided hair floated about her head. Her arms spread, she drifted, gently floating. The current had pulled her down and the struggle was over.

Beams of light pierced the gloom of the water and lit the sea in glowing shafts all around her. Then the sea began to churn and bubble. She was at the last fading moments of consciousness, but she felt herself lifted up. Something was dragging her back to the surface. Suddenly, with hope returning, her lungs were screaming for air again and she was desperate to live, to breathe, to struggle and to survive. She broke the surface, gasping wildly, spluttering and coughing up seawater. Still she rose, up and out of the water. He was there, holding her. It was Sam.

Although his claws were as sharp as knives he held her safe, gently wrapping her in his arms, making sure he didn't press her against the charred, razor-sharp skin that covered his body. He beat his wings and rose slowly into the air. Adda-Leigh looked up and the dragon-boy bent his face towards her.

The sides of his muzzle were covered in denser scales, scalded and damaged and wounded beyond healing, but still delicate in texture. Adda-Leigh raised one long-fingered hand and laid her palm against his cheek. The warmth of his skin ran through her. She felt the touch of his softest breath. No flames, just a deep heat that warmed her frozen body and dried her sodden clothing within moments. She smiled up at him.

'Look at you, Sam! What've you been doing? You're a mess!' She remembered a boy in mud-soaked clothing, just back from the marshes, trying to open the door to his flat with hands too cold to turn the key in the lock.

The great beast closed his one good eye and tipped his head to one side. She heard his voice then. It was the voice she remembered. Sam's human voice. He spoke and the words blossomed in her mind, as clear and as close as if he were whispering in her ear.

'*Adda-Leigh . . .*'

She could hardly bear to hear the sorrow in his voice.

'Sam. Hush. It's okay,' she said, aloud. 'Don't worry. We're here. This is us. You and me. Together at last . . .'

He sighed. *'Time's too short . . .'*

'No. This is our time.' She hardly knew what she was saying. 'It'll last, Sam. We'll make it last.'

They rose through the dusky air, drifting, circling slowly. A flock of seagulls, stunned into unnatural silence by the force of Sam's presence, glided around them like an accompaniment of pale angels. For one brief and fleeting moment, the setting sun burst through the clouds. The sea sparked with a ruby fire. Adda-Leigh and her dragon-boy were illuminated in a shaft of gilded light, as red as the blood in their veins, as rich as their beating hearts.

BEYOND

Sam opened his eye at last, and gazed at Adda-Leigh. But his vision misted and grew faint. His wings folded suddenly and he dropped jerkily down through the air.

'Sam! What is it? Sam!' Adda-Leigh's voice was distant, distorted. But the boat was close by. He could hear Georgette, calling out to them. The strength fled from his limbs and there was a dull ache in his chest. With a desperate effort he managed to slow his descent. He placed Adda-Leigh gently in the boat. Then he fell back into the sea and felt the water close over him.

Someone else was calling now. A man's voice. It was Llew. His dad.

'I'm here, Sam. I'm here. I swam out to the boat.'

'Dad? Dad, I'm glad you're here! I'm not feeling too good. I have to rest for a bit. Can you help?'

All the hurt and bitterness Sam had felt towards his father now dissolved away. This was his dad, Llew the fireman, the hero, coming to the rescue. That was all that mattered.

'You need my help? Well that's what I'm for, see?' Llew's voice was hoarse and he was gasping with the cold, but still he was determined to talk to his son. 'Here to help. That's what I was always for, if only I'd realised it. I'm sorry . . . about everything. How I was when you came to Wales. How I was when you were growing up. I wish I could change the way I was . . .'

'It's okay, Dad. It's okay . . . Listen. I don't think I can get the boat back to shore. You're going to have to do it. Make sure the girls are all right. Make sure Georgette and Adda-Leigh are safe.'

'Of course I will, Sam. You know I will.'

Sam floundered and nearly sank then, thrashing his frozen limbs in the water, but he managed somehow to keep afloat.

'Georgette?'

'Sam?'

'Tell Aaron it was good to see him again. And you, too. You were always so fierce. But I'm glad you were here in the end.'

He swallowed. Flaming bile flared inside his throat, choking him, suffocating him from within.

'*I can't see!*' Everything was dark and he felt a moment of panic. '*Adda-Leigh, are you there? I have to say . . .*'

She interrupted him. 'No. Don't say it . . . you're going to be okay. We can fix you. We can make time. We can . . .' Adda-Leigh's voice trailed off.

Sam heard Georgette then. 'Addy . . . I don't think there's anything we can do.'

But Adda-Leigh wasn't listening. 'Don't you say it, Sam! Don't you say goodbye to me!' Her glistening eyes flashed with anger.

But Sam was too tired to argue. '*All right. I won't.*' His panic subsided. Everything was as it should be.

'That's better.' Adda-Leigh swallowed her tears and smiled as she said his name. 'That's better, Sam Lim-Evans.'

The dragon-boy shivered. His thoughts collapsed in on themselves and he felt as if his mind was turning to stone. But still he formed his final words, barely knowing what they meant any more, other than that they signified something more precious to him than anything else in the world.

'*Adda-Leigh McDuff,*' he said.

Sam sank beneath the waves and felt himself drifting slowly downwards. With the last of his strength he steered his failing bulk out beyond the headland to where the coastal shelf dipped away and the deep water began.

Sam floated down to the dark realm, out of the reach of sunlight. He could feel his skin withering away, scale by scale. Claw and bone, frame and sinew, all dissolved into dust and melted into nothingness.

There had once been an ordinary teenage boy called Sam Lim-Evans, but he'd been lost a long time ago. And now the last of the dragon-folk on earth was about to follow him into the silent land. Beyond all pain, beyond all regret, Sam faded into the shadows of the deep sea and was gone.

GONE

It was too dark to see. The waves broke against the dune. Aaron and Qua and old Mrs Evans waited, sitting in the sand, huddled together for warmth. It wasn't long before the old woman was dozing fitfully. Aaron, however, felt wide awake.

'I expect Sam and his dad will be back soon,' he said to Qua. 'Sam can fly. He'll be able to carry you to the nearest hospital.'

Qua said nothing. His wrist was tightly bound with strips of cloth torn from the lining of Grandma Evans's coat. The bleeding seemed to have stopped. Aaron carried on speaking. He was gripped by the fear that if the old man fell asleep he might never wake up again.

'What about your one, what's-her-name, Fang? Will she be coming back?'

'No. She is gone.' Qua's voice was weak and faltering, but at least he was conscious and didn't seem to be delirious.

'Well I can't say I'm sorry. She sounded like a nasty piece of work.'

But the old man bent his head. His shoulders shook and when he spoke again his voice was hollow with exhaustion. 'Fen was like a daughter to me, and yet I tried to kill her. But still I feel her loss, most keenly, now that she has gone. And gone, too, are my powers. My ability to look into the minds of others, to influence thoughts. Now that Fen is lost to the world, it has all drained away.' He sighed and his tone lightened. 'But it is right that those powers are gone. And Fen was not meant for this world. Perhaps now, everything shall be as it should be.'

Qua lifted his head and turned to Aaron. 'From this day on, I am like you. Just an ordinary person.'

'Who you calling ordinary? Anyway, do me a favour!' Aaron tugged at the sleeve of Qua's robes. Somewhat to his surprise, he felt a surge of sympathy for the old man, even affection. 'There's nothing bog-standard about you, Qua old mate,' Aaron said. 'Never will be. So what are you going to do now, d'you reckon?'

'I don't know.' Qua's voice trembled with dawning amazement. 'For the first time in many years, I truly do not know!'

Aaron wiped his nose with the back of his hand. 'Sounds good. There's a big old world out there.'

'And what of you, Aaron?'

'Me?' Aaron paused for a moment, as if to consider. But his answer was never in doubt. 'I'm going home.'

A signal flare exploded over the headland, dipping through the air, burning a vivid magnesium white against the dark sky. The armed forces were moving in at last.

From out on the water, somewhere close, but hidden in the darkness of the night, there came the sound of weeping.

Qua looked up. 'Listen!' he said. He raised his good hand in a salute to the ink black sky. 'The dragon-folk are no more.'

THE INCIDENT

As darkness fell a Royal Naval frigate arrived offshore, hard by Streaming Point. A group of marine commandos beached their landing craft on the shingle, stormed ashore, then carried out a thorough sweep of the power station and the headland. They found nobody there but the dead.

Over the next few weeks the newspapers, the television, the radio and the Internet, all the world's media, were talking about what quickly became known as 'The Streaming Point Incident'.

According to the authorities, the old power station had been attacked by a group of terrorists, bent on releasing the radioactive waste stored there into the sea. The security team had fought to the last man and had inflicted terrible casualties on the terrorists, actually wiping them all out before they could complete their mission. Although some damage had been done to the nuclear storage building, no contamination of the environment had taken place. But who the terrorists actually were, and what cause they had chosen to die for, was never convincingly explained. None of their dead were ever positively identified.

Of the numerous reports of rocket launchings, unidentified flying objects and radar anomalies noted in the area during the period of the incident, none were ever fully explained. As for the more outlandish claims, of huge reptilian creatures seen battling in Bernardscar or flying over the bay, some suggested they were the product of group hallucinations brought on by a combination of stress and the effects of breathing noxious fumes released from the flooded sewers beneath the village. The only piece of physical evidence, a series of photographs taken on a mobile phone by a man who'd taken refuge in the top floor of the village pub, were so grainy and out of focus that they proved nothing either way.

A handful of civilians who had been overlooked in the initial rescue operation were found by the military and taken to nearby hospitals, all suffering from various injuries, shock and the effects of exposure. Only one, an elderly Oriental man who'd lost a hand during the disaster, was seriously hurt. However, a hospital spokesperson said that, for many of the survivors it would take a long while to recover from the trauma.

If anyone in the corridors of power knew more about the incident than they admitted, they never revealed it. And the village of Bernardscar, evacuated after the terrorists blew the sea wall and flooded the streets in a successful diversionary strike, was eventually restored to its former sleepy glory, following generous donations from the public to a nationwide fund set up for the purpose. A more secure storage facility was found for the nuclear waste kept on Streaming Point. The old power station was left abandoned and empty, ringed by barbed-wire fences and signs warning would-be trespassers of the lingering danger of contamination at the site.

The Streaming Point Incident dominated the headlines but if you'd looked through the inside pages of the newspapers that week you might have come across a report detailing another baffling mystery. The case concerned the disappearance from the laboratories of the department of human archaeology at North-East London University of a two-thousand-year-old corpse. The body of a teenage boy from the Iron Age, recently discovered in a state of perfect preservation in Marshside, London, was apparently stolen sometime during the night that followed the dramatic events on the

Yorkshire coast. There were no signs of a break-in. No clue was ever found as to who may have taken the relic, nor why they may have wanted it. No arrests were ever made. And the preserved body was never recovered.

THE LAST TIME

Sam blinks and looks up. The sun is shining. His injured eye is better. He can see perfectly, and he is no longer in pain.

He shifts his arm, twitches his hand, flexes the fingers. The blood moves in his veins, the air in his lungs. Utterly familiar, and yet strangely new. He feels odd, like he's made out of clay, a figurine of baked earth. But now, as he gulps the air, breathing greedily, the cells in his body seem to flood with life.

There's a small Oriental woman with long black hair standing over him, smiling. He smiles back.

'Don't I know you? Didn't I see you, before? On the sand dune. And over by the petrol station. You were there, weren't you?' He can speak. He is human. He is a boy. Human. He can hardly believe it. Everything is so changed.

The woman nods. 'I watched you in your struggle. And I watched your friends gather around you. I wanted to be sure you wouldn't be alone. I have watched over you all your life, Sam.'

There's something about the way this woman says his name. Sam frowns and tries to think. 'I *do* know you. I'm sure of it.'

The woman pays no attention to this interruption. 'I made a promise that I would be here with you at the very end, to smooth matters out. Things took a very strange turn for you, didn't they, Sam? And you never had any choice in the matter. No choice at all. It broke my heart to see it. It seemed so unfair. So something has been arranged.'

'What kind of something?'

'A one-off.'

'I don't understand.' Sam falls silent. He stares at the woman. 'Wait! I do know who you are. You're . . .'

'Your memory is fading fast, I'm afraid. You can't take it with you, Sam. Not where you're going.'

But Sam is struggling to speak. 'Mum!' Tears burst from his eyes and roll down his cheeks. 'Mum! It's you!'

The woman nods. 'Soon I shall be gone and you will forget. But it's okay, little love. There is no need for me any more. This is a time of transformation, Sam. Of change. Some changes can take a lifetime. Others are achieved in the blink of an eye.'

And Sam blinks.

They were holding him fast, pinning his arms. He didn't want to cry out, but he couldn't help it, not now the moment had come. He knew the place and the people. This was the marsh, his home. And yet he'd never seen any of it before.

Utterly confused, he struggled, shaking his head vigorously from side to side, his black hair falling across his face. But here was the priest, advancing on him with the sacrificial knife in his hand. Death was coming.

Sam blinks again.

The marsh water broke over his head.

Then he was soaked to the skin and shivering, standing outside the locked door to the flat in London, where he and his dad lived. His fingers were too chilled to turn the key in the lock.

Somebody was there. A girl, her skin was pale brown, her features like carved wood. It was Adda-Leigh. It was the first time they'd met outside school. Sam felt the blood shift in his veins. His skin tingled and his heart began to beat. She spoke.

'Oh my days! What happened to you?'

Sam blinks. An Oriental woman is looking down at him. She is smiling, but her eyes are sad. She raises a hand in a gesture of farewell, then she turns and walks away through the straggly marsh grass.

He wants to call out to her. But his voice is little more than a whispered croak, a breath of cold air. He is sure he knows her, but the memory is slipping away, falling from his grasp.

'Who are you?' he says to his mother. It is the last time he will ever see her.

RUSHES AND DAISIES

Marshside, North-East London.
Six Months Later

'There he is, look!'

Georgette looked. Adda-Leigh was gazing at a boy on the other side of the canal. He was around their age, fifteen or sixteen. He was walking through the shimmer and haze of an August afternoon on the marshes. Rushes waved and daisies bowed their heads as he passed by. He somehow managed to look both utterly lost and completely at home. It was a beguiling combination. His jeans were wet up to the knees. An Alsatian puppy danced at his heels, leaping and wagging its tail furiously. The boy's skin was suntanned and his hair was jet black. And there was something about his eyes, about the way he moved.

It was the summer holiday. Georgette was staying with her father at his new flat in Lambeth, helping him get ready for the grand opening of his cafe and bar. But she'd taken a day off to visit Adda-Leigh.

They'd gone for a walk on the marsh. This was where Georgette had once ridden Dandelion, the horse. It was where Sam had first felt the effects of the transformation that was to overtake him. Where Adda-Leigh and Aaron had gone in search of the dragon-boy, in the dark of a winter night. This was where it had all begun. The marsh was a place that would stay with them for ever.

And now there was this boy and his dog, walking through the long grass.

'What's his name?' Georgette said to Adda-Leigh.

'That's just it, nobody knows. Even he doesn't know. They found him wandering on the marsh. Lost his memory. No one's been able to identify him. You must have heard about it, he's been on the national news and everything.'

Georgette shook her head. She tended to avoid the news these days. There was no need to worry about the Order. They were gone. Instead, Georgette concentrated all her attention on the people that were close to her, her family, her friends, the people she loved.

She'd been very worried about Adda-Leigh. It was only now that her friend was anything like her old self again. But she was definitely getting better. She'd even regained some of the weight she'd lost after what had happened on Streaming Point. This was the first time in six months that she'd shown much interest in anything at all.

'He's staying in a foster home near here. He goes to St Michael's, he's in my year. That's how I know him.'

Georgette watched the boy as he crossed the bridge, heading towards them. Now that she'd seen him, she wasn't too surprised that he'd caught Adda-Leigh's attention. Although he didn't really look like a half-Oriental, half-Welsh boy, there was still something about him that reminded Georgette of Sam Lim-Evans.

A dragonfly flashed across the canal, dipping its electric-blue body at the dark water and rippling the still of the surface. The insect rose high. It hovered in the air, a tiny speck against the pale turquoise sky.

Adda-Leigh leaned against one of the concrete bollards on the towpath and tried to look casual. Georgette had to smile. The boy walked past and darted a look at Adda-Leigh.

'Hi,' said the boy.

'Hi,' said Adda-Leigh.

THE MARSH SLEEPS

It is past two o'clock in the morning. Out on the marshes a shroud of mist hangs over the waterlogged ground. There's a calmness in the shifting grass and the dark pools. In the shadow of the railway embankment, the burnt-out skeleton of a long-abandoned car rusts quietly. The night air shifts and the urban wetland seems to breathe a deep sigh. Something has been lost. Something has been returned.